Feig

Richard D. Bank

PS
BOOKS
Regional Publishing, National Voice
A division of Philadelphia Stories

Feig
by Richard D. Bank

Feig Copyright © 2014 Richard D. Bank
Published by PS Books, a division of Philadelphia Stories, Inc.
First PS Books edition, 2014

ISBN 978-0-9793350-7-5

Cover Images: "Prison Cell at Terezin" © Marco Restano; "Roundhouse, Philadelphia" © Vinny Natale
Cover Design: Sarah Eldridge
Book Design: Sarah Eldridge

PS Books
93 Old York Road
Ste. 1-753
Jenkintown, PA 19046
www.psbookspublishing.org

For Hayden and Rebecca
and their Granny Frani,
my *bashert*, my soulmate.

1

The first time I saw Feig was at the Health Club. I saw him there often in the months that followed, but I'd also see him in other, less auspicious, surroundings. I'd see him emerge from the lockup, panting like a caged animal, his beady eyes glaring at those who sought dominion over his body and soul. I'd hear his heels clicking across the courtroom's scuffed floors and watch him, shoulders squared, the knuckles of his brawny hands still white from gripping the black bars that imprisoned him. The last time I saw Feig, he was soaring into the heavens like the mythical phoenix, purplish wings merging with the red-yellow light of the rising sun.

But all of that was yet to come. When I met Feig at the Health Club it had been over fifteen years since my father had given me the membership as a law school graduation gift. I think the Health Club reminded him of the club he had belonged to when he was a younger man building his own business.

Every Wednesday night when I was a boy, my father joined his buddies at "the *schvitz*," a three-story concrete building called Camac after the narrow cobblestone street on which it sat in Center City Philadelphia. In post-Depression America, where hunger pangs and bread lines were not yet a distant memory, men like my father labored mightily to put food on the table. Camac was my father's respite from a sixty-hour workweek selling houses to World War II veterans relying on VA mortgages.

In Camac, men with white sheets draped over their fleshy naked torsos strutted like preening peacocks from the steam rooms to the swimming pool to the dairy bar's counter, where they plumped their rumps on red vinyl stools and devoured blintzes and borscht and peaches slathered in sour cream. After rinsing the sweat that streamed from their unclogged pores in the steam rooms, they might meander to the poker and pinochle tables. There the aroma of tobacco wafted from well-chewed cigars, freshly-stoked pipes, and cigarettes dangling from slackened lips.

Occasionally I'd accompany my father to Camac and, once I turned twelve, I was allowed to lift the barbells and dumbbells in the weight room and shoot hoops or ricochet the ball off the walls of the handball court. But by the age of fifteen I had decided that tagging along with my father and his friends at Camac was no longer cool. After he'd heard a few of my lame excuses, my father stopped asking if I wanted to join him. By the time I passed the bar exam and joined the District Attorney's Office, Camac had closed. So my beaming father presented me with a receipt for a one-year membership at the Health Club.

Like my father's gym, the Health Club was for men only. It was a miniature version of Camac without the dairy bar and basketball and handball courts. But the Health Club featured a weight room and stationary bikes, a sleeping room with reclining chairs, a massage room, and even a small swimming pool that could accommodate two or three men doing laps. There was also a steam room, where members could lounge and perspire. I always worried that those who caught catnaps there might fall into a deep sleep and cook to death. I never allowed myself to nod off. When beads of perspiration stung our eyes, we filled a bucket and poured cold water over our heads. The bucket of cold water required proper etiquette, however. It pissed me off when some fool splashed icy water everywhere, drenching some unsuspecting soul in repose on the bench.

It was there in the steam room that I first saw Jacob Feig. I had doused the tiles with water to cool them off and was lying on the bench when I heard the door swing open. I craned my neck and lifted one eyelid. A man of about sixty, a stranger, sloshed into the room.

I lolled my head back and shut my eyes. Neither of us said a word. I wasn't being unfriendly; I wanted to rest. I heard him fill the bucket and knew he was only a few feet away when icy water trickled under my calves.

The bucket clanged as he dropped it on the floor. He should have placed it back under the spigot, of course, but I assumed he was new and so excused this lapse of protocol. I heard more splashing and the squishing of his ass settling onto the tiles. A few minutes later, I sat up.

The stranger was of slight build, but something about him—perhaps his firm abdomen or prominent biceps—exuded strength. The dark gray hair on his head matched the tufts on his chest. His chiseled face and Roman nose gave him a severe look, but a glint in his soft azure eyes intrigued me.

"How ya doin'," I said.

"Hello." This single word revealed a hint of an accent, perhaps European.

"New here?"

"Yes. My wife purchased a membership for me as a present," he said, discharging each word like a pellet from a BB gun. "We don't live close but my job is nearby. When I can, I will come after work."

"What is it you do?"

"I work in the maintenance department of an elementary school," he said. "I'm quite good with my hands."

We both looked down at the blotchy red backs of his hands, dry and crisscrossed with protruding veins. His palms, I knew, would be callused and tough. They were hands with a history, with character, and with a story to tell.

"Ilse, my wife, is not well," the man went on. "I must care for her. There is the social security—something left from her first husband—but it goes only so far. With this job I can make ends meet and, since I finish at four, I can shop and take Ilse to the doctor or run errands." He wiped his forehead and gazed around the steam room. "And now I can come here."

I can't say exactly what fascinated me about him initially. Perhaps it was something about his voice, about what he did not say.

He edged toward me and extended his hand. "My name is Feig. Jacob Feig."

"David Gold," I said. I winced at his vice-like grip.

"Gold? The name is familiar," said Feig. He knit his bushy eyebrows together.

"I don't know why. Unless we've had some dealings. I'm an attorney."

"An attorney? No, it is something else."

"Maybe—" I hesitated. "Maybe you've read some of my book reviews?"

"Yes, that is it!" Feig said. "The *Jewish Exponent*. I read your reviews, but there are not many."

Tact, I would soon learn, was not Feig's strong suit. "That's because I'm a freelancer," I said. "The *Exponent* spreads the assignments around."

Unlike most people, who lose interest when they learn that I'm not an attorney-turned-famous-novelist like John Grisham or Scott Turow, Feig remained intrigued. "You also write things other than reviews, no?" Feig narrowed his eyes.

"Occasionally," I said. Two drawers in my file cabinet at home were filled with manuscripts—poems, short stories, essays, book proposals, and even a novel. Some rejected, but most never sent out.

"You just wrote something about your grandparents and *Kristallnacht*."

I nodded. *Kristallnacht* was the infamous "night of the broken glass." On November 9, 1938, Hitler unleashed a swarm of stormtroopers and anti-Semitic thugs to rampage and ravish the Third Reich's Jews. The vision of my grandparents fleeing the home they would never see again still haunted me as the fiftieth anniversary approached, so I had written about it.

"What became of your grandparents?" he asked.

"They moved around from one place to another until 1942. Then they were sent to Theresienstadt."

Feig arched his back and squared his shoulders. "And after that?" He knew how slim the chances were that my grandparents would have avoided transport to Auschwitz and death.

"They survived," I said. I did not believe, as my mother did, that we had God to thank for sparing Ludwig and Sophie.

Feig leaned in so close that I could smell the dankness in his hair. "I, too, am a survivor, you know," he said in a hushed, almost conspiratorial, tone. There was a defiant glitter in his eyes.

His disclosure startled me. Perhaps it was because he seemed so unlike the other survivors I had encountered. And it wasn't just his accent. The others rolled "r's" off their tongues that slipped through thin lips as snakelike hisses, their "h's" were harsh, guttural, and deep, and their "ch's" transmogrified into rocklike "k's" that crushed any inkling of empathy or kindness.

These survivors sometimes visited my mother and her parents in the home where I grew up. The men were stiff and proper, their collars starched over tightly-knotted ties. The women wore wide-brimmed hats that shadowed their faces and hid their eyes. Their full-length dresses ended at thickset ankles shrouded by heavy brown stockings. Sitting straight in hardback mahogany chairs, the women sipped tea while the men drank their coffee black and smoked half-filled pipes or cheap stubby cigars.

These were the survivors I had known. Distant relatives three and four times removed. Friends of friends from Europe. Acquaintances of acquaintances. And our close family? Murdered in the Shoah. Almost all of my mother's aunts, uncles, and cousins were killed. The few who did survive, like my mother, fled to safer shores before the conflagration made escape impossible.

Besides my grandparents, the only family member who survived the killing camps was a cousin, Ernst, who was a child at the time of the Holocaust. By the time I knew Ernst he was aged beyond his years. He shuffled along, humpbacked, continually brushing sparse grayish-brown hair off his high forehead so he could peer through thick glasses that made his jet-black eyes look like they were bulging from their sockets. But Ernst never spoke of his travails, and I only learned that he had been in Auschwitz when the rabbi delivered a brief eulogy at his funeral.

And my grandparents? They reached America's shores shortly before I was born. When I was old enough to wonder about them and summon the courage to ask where these people who spoke almost no English had come from, my mother's glare or a wave of dismissal or even a kick under the table quickly shushed me. It was as though her parents had flown on a magic carpet from a strange and distant land shrouded in secrecy.

Eventually I learned that there was a period of time—from just before my mother emigrated to the United States to shortly before my birth—that was not to be discussed. And these years remained a *verboten* topic After both my grandparents were dead, my mother feigned no memory of this time. I learned nothing from firsthand, or even secondhand, testimony about the life my grandparents led behind the ramparts of the ghetto where they were confined and remained for the course of the War. When they emerged from under Terezin's stone archway, stooped and hollow, they began a tortuous journey to America. Here, living with my parents and me, their narrative continued and we could speak of it.

Until Feig, I had never met a survivor who was willing to speak freely about the Holocaust. And so I was drawn to this enigmatic figure who seemed willing to share his story. We sat so close on the dripping tile bench that his thigh occasionally brushed mine. "What was it like?" I asked.

He said nothing at first, and I was afraid I had misread him. Would he remain silent like all the others? Would the Shoah remain an elusive phantasm accessible only through secondary sources? But then I saw the twinkle in his eyes and, after a moment, he spoke.

"Somehow, you know, I found myself alive when Auschwitz was hastily emptied in advance of the Russian 'hordes' as the Germans called them. And who is to say why a few lived while so many died?" Feig parted his lips but did not smile. "I was on one of the last death marches out of Auschwitz—we were mostly the sick, the old, and the young—

destined for Germany. Those of us who avoided starving or freezing to death or being shot or bludgeoned by a guard along the journey would join the other Jews gathered there for the final slaughter."

Feig stared through me. I looked down and saw the purplish numbers tattooed on his forearm. How could I have missed such a thing? I'd concentrated on his hands for so long. It wasn't the first time, nor would it be the last time, that I failed to see something I didn't want to see that was right in front of me all along.

As much as I yearned to know more, I remained silent. I had been well trained. Did I detect a mocking glint in his blue eyes, daring me to ask about the dark secrets concealed behind his gaze? I wiped the sweat from my brow.

"We'll speak of this another time," Feig said. "When you're not so hot." His smirk bared yellowish teeth.

"Yes," I said as I stood up. "I'm maxed. Good to meet you. I'm sure I'll see you around."

Since we were both in the habit of arriving at the Health Club late in the afternoon, I often glanced into the gym as I signed in at the front desk and saw Feig in the gym working out with the concentration of a Zen master. He avoided the machines and kept to the free weights. He used the dumbbells for curls and triceps extensions and the barbell for presses. He rarely asked for a spotter, but whenever I saw him at the bench press I offered to spot. Standing above him and peering down with my hands hovering just over the bar for two sets of ten reps, I was impressed with the determination in his jaw as he inhaled and exhaled, his wide nostrils flaring like a raging bull. Just as the bar was about to land on his sinewy chest, it snapped back and climbed upward until his arms were fully extended. Not until the final rep, when

the bar teetered a little, did it appear he was even remotely
in need of aid. On the few occasions I moved to grab the bar
Feig shooed me off with a grunt. He always finished the set
himself.

But Feig was a different man in the steam room.
At the first blast of steam, the intensity with which he had
exercised vanished and his square shoulders and taut body
relaxed. After cooling the tiles, splashing his face, and sliding
the empty bucket back to the spigot (he did learn the protocol), he exhaled and closed his eyes. He sat in silence unless
he wanted to say something—like the day he began to tell me
about his life in Europe.

As eager as I was to hear him talk about the Shoah, I
had not asked him. It was his story, and I had no right. Somehow I knew he would get to it in his own time. Being the
orderly man he was, there was only one place to start his tale.
At the beginning.

"I lived in the Carpathian Mountains, David, in a
small village called Sighet that was then part of Hungary,"
Feig said. "Does that sound familiar?" He smiled. He knew
I would recognize the name because I had reviewed several
books by Elie Wiesel, the Nobel Laureate who had grown up
in Sighet.

"Did you know Wiesel?" I asked. He cocked his head
and shrugged, preferring to preserve the mystery as he continued his story.

"The Nazis did not cross the border into Hungary
until March, 1944, you know. They did this because they
needed a bigger labor force. Also, they were running out of
Jews to murder and Hungary had more than three quarter of
a million fresh victims. Hitler installed a puppet regime to
secure labor and round up Jews to be killed."

"Didn't the Hungarian Jews have some idea what was in store for them?" I asked. I knew that almost two-thirds of Hungarian Jewry had perished at the hands of the Nazis in a single year—after the War's outcome had been decided and when the world was aware of the death camps. So I'd always wondered how these Jews could not have been aware of the genocide.

"What did we know, David? Most of us were simple people living in small towns like Sighet. Oh yes, there were rumors." Feig gazed into the steam. "I remember a man—not of Sighet—a stranger who appeared one day out of nowhere. He frightened me. He looked like a walking skeleton. I never saw such a man before. His eyes bulged from their sockets and his skin was jaundiced, dry, and cracked. He was so frail that I feared the wind would blow him away. He hovered in the shadows outside one of the *shuls* on Shabbat and begged everyone to run away. 'Run?' people asked him. 'Run to where?' 'Anywhere!' he shouted.

"This ghost of a man told us of places where the Germans gassed Jews by the thousands every day—all day, all night. He spoke of shootings and hangings and of mothers so desperate they threw their babies onto electric wires to spare them the suffering.

"'*Mishugeneh!*' the rabbi screamed at this man. 'You should be ashamed of yourself, frightening people with such nonsense!' But the man did not recant. He did not take back a single syllable of what he had said. Instead, he roamed from house to house, like a phantom in the night, telling the same stories over and over in the voice of one who has seen hell and returned to tell others.

"But no one took him seriously and so finally, one morning, he was gone. Perhaps off to some other village to warn the Jews living there. 'He was a madman,' everyone agreed. But he wasn't mad, was he, David?" Feig's thin lips twisted.

As if he could hear my thoughts, he continued. "Before you criticize the Jews of Sighet for not heeding this man, tell me, David, would you have believed him? Would you have abandoned all your worldly belongings? Left the place that had been home to your family for generations? Would you have believed, even imagined in your worst nightmares, that a place like Auschwitz could actually exist?"

I had no answer. I had asked myself this question many times. How could my grandparents and most of their family have stayed in Germany until it was too late?

"But the world knew," Feig growled. "They knew, all right. They had proof. The Allies could have bombed the rails, you know, leading into Auschwitz, the trains transporting Jews to their deaths. But they did not do this." Feig's eyes blazed. I was afraid he might smash his clenched fist into the tiled bench. But he regained his composure and continued his tale.

"My father was only a clothing merchant, but he travelled and he was a smart man. He could see it was safer to live in Budapest than in villages and towns like Sighet where one day there were Jews and the next day the Nazis and Hungarian gendarmes swooped down and marched off all the Jews. Not one Jew would be spared, David, not one." Feig stared into my eyes and I shifted in discomfort. I was grateful when he continued.

"So my father decided that we would move to Budapest. Arrangements had to be made. I had just been bar mitzvahed and was considered a man, so it was agreed that I would accompany my father to Budapest. It was my first trip to a big city. I couldn't believe what I saw—the tall buildings, cobbled streets, trolleys, and motorcars. People seated at tables outside the cafes and eating food. Imagine, tea and cake in the middle of the day! And dressed in such fine clothes—like it was Shabbat! But it wasn't Shabbat. And the Jews, David—ah, Jews like I had never seen before. They wore no hats or *yarmulkes*, and their earlocks and beards were gone. They looked just like the *goyim*! Except for the Stars of David on their coats.

"Soon after we arrived, gendarmes came out of no-where. They ran everywhere, blowing whistles and barking orders. They grabbed Jews wearing the yellow star, threw them into the street, and ordered them to stay where they fell. They tossed my father and me down with them. My father had heard of such things, but I had no idea what was going on—that a mustering of Jewish men and boys had be-gun to form a labor force for Hitler. Slave labor like the He-brews in Egypt—only this German pharaoh was worse, much worse, and this time God did not deliver us from bondage."

I shrank back into the tiles as Feig glowered.

"So, my father and I were dispatched to 110/319 work brigade of the Jewish Forced Labor Service. We never saw Sighet or my mother and sister again." Feig looked away.

I felt woozy and my skin was on fire. Was it the story or the steam? I'd never stayed in the steam room for so long. I had to escape.

Feig grasped my forearm to steady me as I stood. "Thanks," I mumbled. "I'd better get out before I pass out." He nodded and smiled as a father might smile at his young son who couldn't handle the steam.

"I'll tell you more, David," he said. "There is more to tell. And, who knows, maybe you will write of it Yes?"

I turned to look back at Feig. He was smiling.

2

In 1937, at the age of seventeen, my mother boarded a ship bound for America. Her parents saw her off at the dock, but no one dared utter the word "goodbye"—as if saying it aloud would make it come true. Instead, they treated this parting as if my mother were going on another weekend excursion to visit her grandparents. Many years later, this is how my mother described the scene.

Stiff upper lips. No tears, no hugs, no kisses—never in public. Forced smiles. A father's understanding nod of the head. A mother's touch on the shoulder. An adolescent girl's quivering lips and anxious glance at the swelling throng slowly making its way up the gangplank.

Eight years later, another ship crossed the Atlantic with two survivors of Hitler's Holocaust in its hull. Faces gaunt, they disembarked in New York with shoulders drooping, shuffling forward, nearly unrecognizable shadows of their former selves. One frayed black suitcase between them held all their worldly possessions.

The day that my mother learned her parents were alive there was no telegram, no phone call, no dramatic visit from an official anxious to bear good tidings. There was only an innocuous looking envelope that she set aside, unopened, while she sorted through the bills. But when she slit open the envelope and removed the letter, her fingers began to tremble as she scanned the page. And she let out a scream so loud a neighbor came running to see if she was all right.

The message, issued by the German Jewish Representative Committee, was dated July 1945. It read:

> Dear Friends
>
> *We are happy to inform you that we have just received from the offices of the World Jewish Congress in London a message for their*

daughter living in Philadelphia that
Ludwig Frank and
Sophie Frank
has been found among the survivors of Theresienstadt.

If no address has been mentioned above, we are sorry that it is not
possible, for the time being, to get in touch with your relatives
liberated in Theresienstadt.

The form letter wasn't signed, nor did it provide further information. My mother didn't sleep that night. Early the next morning, she was packed and ready to leave for New York, where the Jewish agencies were located. My father drove her to the train station, gave her all the money in his wallet for a train ticket and a hotel room, and marveled at the spring in her step when she alighted from the car. Her eyes glistened when she turned back, leaned into the car, and kissed my father on the mouth. She tossed her jet-black hair, smiled, swiveled, and sprinted off. "Is this the woman I married?" my father must have asked himself. "Where has she been all this time?"

Three days later, my father came home from work to find his wife dancing around the apartment, ripping open cartons of fresh bed sheets and blankets to set up the guestroom. She ran to my father, hugged him, and beamed. The guestroom is temporary, she promised. They would make another arrangement. My mother had insisted on not starting a family until she knew her parents' fate but now, she said, the time had come. It might have been the happiest day in my parents' lives.

Less than two years after my grandparents arrived in the United States, I was born into a household of four adults—two of whom could not speak English. We spoke German during the day until my father, who did not speak German, came home from work. Family conversations were a cacophony of English, Yiddish, and German.

Until I was five years old, my parents and I lived on the ground floor of a triplex in a middle-class neighborhood across the street from Fairmount Park. Though my grandparents occupied the second-floor apartment, we took our meals together and moved freely between the two apartments.

My grandfather took me to the park several times a week. We'd walk to the corner and wait for the traffic signal to turn. He'd grasp my hand and squeeze so hard that it sometimes hurt. But I didn't complain. Once the light changed in our favor, he'd look back and forth furtively before cautiously leading me across the intersection, treading carefully as if walking through a minefield. Only after we reached the other side did he loosen his grip.

The park stretched as far as I could see. There was an endless expanse where picnickers spread their blankets and set up lawn chairs so they could read and talk and lunch. Men, and occasionally a few women, volleyed balls over the nets on the tennis courts. There were swings, seesaws, and slides but, according to my grandfather, they were *verboten* to me. My mother upheld my grandfather's injunction. "Too dangerous until you're older," she said.

My grandfather clutched me by the collar until we reached the top of the grassy knoll we usually had all to ourselves. Then he would wink and let go. I'd take off like a wild pony, bridled only by my grandfather's vigilant gaze.

I loved the colors of the park—green grass and shrubs, flowers of every hue, the bright clothes people wore, and especially the whites of the tennis players. As long as I kept my grandfather in sight I knew he could see me. His color was gray. He always wore his charcoal overcoat or, if it was a mild day, his steel-gray suit and matching felt hat.

When we weren't in the park, Opa spent the afternoons sitting on our porch, smoking a pipe, and reading *Aufbau*, a newspaper written in German for German-speaking Jews. Sometimes I'd jump up on his lap and he'd bounce his leg. Other times I'd help him stuff his pipe. When he opted for a cigar, he'd hand me the ring that he stripped off the cellophane wrapper and I'd wear it on my thumb.

My friends called their grandparents *bubbe* and *zayde* or grandma and grandpa, but I referred to mine as *oma* and *opa*. Later, when I used this affectionate German idiom in front of my friends, they would stare at me curiously. It was one of the many things that made me feel different and strange once I started school and began to see a new horizon beyond the boundaries of my home and backyard.

I was born in America and I spoke English like everyone else, though I also communicated in a rudimentary German with my grandparents. Being bilingual had the unintended effect of replacing the prevalent Philadelphia nasal twang with a long "a," which made me sound like a snooty New Englander. When I became a bit older and entered grade school, I tried to mitigate the teasing by avoiding words with "a's"—not an easy task. But this discomfiture was nothing compared to the way I felt when one or both of my grandparents followed me in the streets of the neighborhood. At such times, I wanted to burrow into the ground and disappear.

Opa always kept an eye on me. At the first sign of any real or imagined danger—a speeding car, a ball thrown too hard, or maybe a "gang" of *schvartzers* (children of the "Negro" families who had begun moving into the neighborhood)—Opa leapt from his rocker. He'd lumber toward me in his suit, starched white shirt, tie, and hat, waving his cane to fend off whatever evil was threatening to befall his only grandson.

Oma's concerns largely had to do with warding off sickness and disease. At the first sign of a darkening sky or ominous clouds Oma, raincoat in hand, tracked me down. She snapped all the fasteners and pulled the hood so far down I could barely see. Cold weather brought Oma running to dress me in gloves, scarf, and a heavy jacket. In the heat, my stomach bloated and my bladder felt ready to burst with all the water she made me drink. One sneeze or a cough and she'd plop the thermometer into my mouth, her fretting face so close I could see the creases on her forehead and hear her anxious breathing. She had even tried to keep me from starting school. My parents sent me off to nursery school, but after a week of my tears and feigning sickness and Oma's insistence that I should not go, my mother gave in and kept me home that extra year.

Much as I wanted to shoo my grandparents away and beg them not to embarrass me in public, I always blushed, lowered my head, and permitted them to dote and hover over me. Although I could not have imagined how every other hope had been wrested from them in the worst way imaginable, at some level I did understand that I was their future.

I carried this responsibility as both an honor and an obligation. Only decades later, the glitter in Feig's azure eyes—blue like Opa's—forced me to acknowledge what their good intentions and well-meaning concern had cost me.

My father, meanwhile, had become ever more convinced that success was bound to come with hard work. He relocated his real estate office to the northern boundary of Philadelphia and built five houses there. He kept one ranch house for us and sold the other four at a handsome profit.

In this new house, a ranch, there was one bedroom for my parents, one for Oma and Opa, and one for me. We lived there until after my bar mitzvah. I loved that house. It felt as though we had transplanted a bit of Fairmount Park in the woods behind the house. I spent many happy hours exploring uncharted wilderness like Davy Crockett and Daniel Boone. I even had a coonskin cap like the one Davy wore on TV. As I wriggled through the dense underbrush and traipsed through my territory, the canopy of intertwining branches shaded me from reality. I was free to roam undisturbed. Neither of my grandparents had any inclination to tramp through the thicket to follow me.

A few years later, however, houses were constructed on the site and my woodland adventures were over. The new houses were, like most of the other homes in the neighborhood, row houses and twins—unlike our single ranch house. Our house was one more thing that set me apart.

But, different as our houses looked on the outside, I felt even more out of place when I stepped inside a friend's house. These were boisterous houses filled with laughter, loud voices, and sometimes even yelling. The aroma of freshly baked cake or cookies would lure us into the kitchen where we'd gorge ourselves on the treats after pouring some milk from the refrigerator. When I was invited for lunch, we'd drink soda and eat potato chips with our bologna or salami sandwiches with mustard on rye bread. Afterwards, my friends' moms might dip some ice cream out of a carton in the freezer.

My house was silent. My friends spoke in hushed voices, assuming people were asleep. They hated the sandwiches my mother fixed—lots of lettuce and tomato with fresh turkey breast or tuna dripping with mayonnaise served between thin slices of black pumpernickel that fell apart with the first bite. Oma believed that ice cream and soda were bad for the teeth, and my mother scorned potato chips as "junk." Until my father set up a ping-pong table in the basement, mine was the house of last resort.

I was conscious of other differences, too. The mantels and tables in my friends' homes displayed framed photographs of their parents, often dressed as bride and groom. Many also had a picture of a man in a uniform. Almost all of my friends' fathers fought in World War II. Other people's houses had pictures of the extended family, too—grandparents, uncles, aunts, and cousins. On the stone mantel above the fireplace in my house there was one photo—of my parents and me.

My friends never saw the photograph Oma kept by her bed, or the other that sat in a corner of a bookshelf in her bedroom. The first, on her night table, was faded and set in a simple silver frame. In the foreground were five people sitting on chairs, and four men with dark hair stood behind them. An old man with a white beard sat in the center, with a gray-haired woman to his right. Three young women, their backs straight and hands folded primly on their laps, sat in the other chairs. They all reminded me of my mother. Nine pairs of eyes focused on the camera. No one was smiling.

"*Mein Vater und meine Mutter, meine Geschwestern*," Oma explained as she pointed at the photo. I had never met any of these people. I didn't know their names or anything about them. As much as I wanted to learn more, something kept me from asking about them. This pattern, of squelching my innate curiosity, was woven into my personality. If I was supposed to know something, I would be told. Some things, I deduced, are better left unsaid.

Years later, when I was college, this photo became the center of Oma's universe. Senility had set in and her already thin and weakened body had become even frailer and so, reluctantly, my mother arranged for Oma to live out her final years in a home for the aged. I visited my grandmother once a week and, though I always scurried down the gauntlet of wheelchair-lined corridors, I was never fast enough to escape the haunting guilt impressed on me by the glaring wizened faces of their occupants. As though I were responsible for their plight.

Once I finally reached Oma's room at the end of the hall, though, I was back in her bedroom at home. Her personal belongings filled the room—most notably the photograph of her family, which sat on her nightstand Several times during each visit, she would point to the photo and tell me that her sisters and brothers were all living in Israel. I would nod and smile, not daring to remind her they were all long dead—murdered by the Nazis.

The other photo, the one that had been on the bookshelf in Oma and Opa's bedroom, was of two young men dressed in the uniform of German officers in World War I. Their faces were proud, with coal-black mustaches over firmly-set lips. Opa, who stood a head taller, rested his hand on his younger brother's shoulder.

What I saw in this picture was yet another piece of family history that set me apart. Most of my friends' fathers fought in World War II, but my dad failed the physical because he had had tuberculosis (which had killed his own father). I also had to make sure no one found out that, in the First World War, my forebears fought on the opposing side. My ignominious military heritage might not have been so terrible for a boy to bear today, but in the 1950s, when the country had elected a military leader as its president, it was not something to make public. World War II was a constant topic

of conversation among my friends, who bragged about their
fathers' war exploits and showed off their helmets and army
jackets. At school, whenever Veterans Day or Memorial Day
approached or the subject was World War II, I'd slink down in
my seat and pray that the teacher wouldn't call on me to talk
about my family. The more I learned, the more complex the
issues became. It was because of Opa's distinguished service
and injuries sustained for the *Vaterland* that my grandparents
were sent to Theresienstadt and spared an early dispatch to the
death camps.

I had my first inkling that there was something unique
about my grandparents—something beyond the foreign
language they spoke and the fact that they rarely went out or
received visitors—after an incident in second grade. I had
finished lunch at home and was heading back to school when,
suddenly, the clouds formed a bluish-gray dome, lightning
flashed, and thunder roared. All of the kids clambered for
cover. I was huddled under a maple tree waiting for a break
from the torrential downpour when I felt a tug at my shoulder. I turned and cringed. There was Oma, holding an um-
brella over her head and my yellow vinyl raincoat in her other
hand. Without a word, she began slipping it on me. I held my
arm tight against my side, resisting as best I could, but she was
determined.

"*Gey vecht!*" I shouted, looking around to see if my
friends were watching. "*Gey vecht!*" But Oma did not retreat
and she persisted. I pushed at her and screamed for her to go
away. When I turned to make a run for it, my face collided
with the ample midsection of my teacher, Miss Schneider. Her
eyes burned with the stare she gave the most unruly students
before dispatching them to the stool in the corner. Arms folded across her chest, she stood blocking my escape route.

"Remain where you are, David," she commanded. She nodded at my grandmother. I obeyed, and Oma put on my slicker.

"*Danke*," Oma said to Miss Schneider. Miss Schneider smiled at her. They spoke for a moment in German and, when they parted, Miss Schneider glared down at me over the frames of her horn-rimmed glasses. She clucked her tongue, frowned, and ordered me back to school.

Miss Schneider commanded me to stand before the class. I slouched up to her desk, freckled face beet red, wondering what I had done wrong.

"Children, learn a lesson from David Gold!" Miss Schneider said. "I never want to see any of you do what he did today."

When I heard a muffled guffaw, I clenched my fists and raised my head. Every set of eyes was on Miss Schneider and I couldn't identify the source of the snickers. Miss Schneider told everyone about the terrible thing I had done. "David Gold yelled at his grandmother, a refugee from Europe, a woman who spent time in a concentration camp!"

I lowered my head again when I saw the girls' wide-eyed disdain and shock, but not before I had spotted Michelle. Until that moment, her blond hair and sparkling blue eyes had filled me with the hope she would be my first girlfriend. My hopes were dashed.

None of us knew about concentration camps, but Miss Schneider made it clear it was a bad place to have been. "We must pity David's unfortunate grandmother," she said. "She deserves better than the disrespectful treatment she received from her impudent grandson."

As punishment, I sat on the stool in the corner during recess for a week. Miss Schneider sat behind her desk peering down at papers, and every so often she'd glance up, cluck her tongue, and glower over her horn-rimmed glasses. I was a boy who had been callous and cruel to his poor grandmother.

Every German word my grandparents spoke, and every word my mother uttered in her heavily accented English, whether in our home when a friend was there or, worse, out in public, reminded me that there was something profoundly foreign about my family. I knew the world was a dangerous place and that, if one wasn't cautious, something harmful would happen. I didn't know exactly what that calamity was and it was only decades later, after Feig came into my life, that I dared to ask.

3

Even now, Miss Schneider's reprimand comes back
to haunt me. One afternoon I was lying on a recliner at the
Health Club, steamed and showered and relaxed, when memory caught me unaware. I felt the heat rise to my face as my
stomach sank and, in an instant, I was back in that classroom
hearing the boys' guffaws and enduring the girls' disdainful
glares as Miss Schneider exposed my crime.

I lay still, with my eyes closed, and searched for an
escape from my shame through other stories. I was an adult
before my mother told me about her childhood. She was so
reticent to talk about herself that I think she only told me
when she did because she'd reached a point at which looking
back seemed better than staring ahead into old age—even
when the past held so much pain.

Still, I knew she did not tell me everything. She
would catch herself mid-sentence and the tale would take
a ninety-degree turn. Or her eyelids would flutter like the
wings of a baby bird, as if she were attempting to blink away
something she didn't want to see, something she'd rather
forget.

Often her stories would begin by setting the scene at
her family home in Germany. The house was so large that my
grandparents employed staff to tend to the house and its gardens and grounds. My grandmother insisted on lush gardens
displaying a spectrum of colors in each new season. She also
made sure that everything was tidy and well maintained.

These caretakers remained faceless and nameless
characters in the background of my mother's tales except
for Hilda, the cook. Hilda was a rotund middle-aged matron

with a characteristic bright crimson blush. She had never married and doted on my mother as if she were her own daughter. Hilda was such a good cook that my grandmother never prepared meals but only instructed Hilda what to make, and for how many, and informed her whether it was a night for regular dishes or for the better china to impress guests.

Sometimes these honored guests were the town gentry—the mayor with his well-waxed upturned mustache and penchant for good schnapps, the stern and humorless headmaster of the gymnasium where my mother was enrolled, or the rabbi of the synagogue where the family attended weekly Shabbat services. More often than not, however, the person sitting at the head of the table opposite my grandfather was a traveling peddler selling wares, or a gaunt Talmudic student headed for a distant center of learning, or an unkempt vagabond with nowhere to go. Without fail, once or twice a week, and always on Shabbat eve, someone in need of a meal found himself at my grandmother's table. All of the villagers directed such inquiring wayfarers to my grandmother because they knew she would never turn anyone away.

All of the neighbors required commoners to enter through the back door, but my grandmother would have none of it. Whenever she hired someone new, she made it crystal clear that everyone entered through the front door—no exceptions. "*Verstehen?*" she would ask, looking the new gardener or maid straight in the eye. Everyone in the household understood that strangers were to be treated with dignity and respect. Their jackets or coats were taken and hung in the closet, and they were ushered into the sitting room for a pre-dinner drink with my grandfather.

Feig

The kindness my grandmother extended to people flowed from her commitment to the teachings and commandments of Torah. Her treatment of animals, though, stemmed from a deep and genuine love for them. Every family member, employee, and guest knew never to throw away leftover food. Scraps were saved, placed on plates, and set out in the backyard for stray cats, squirrels, birds, raccoons, and even a possum or two. My grandmother also instructed the staff to replenish saucers of milk and water every day. As my mother described all this to me, she would say with a sparkle in her eyes that the backyard looked more like a menagerie than the well-tended gardens of one of the town's celebrated horticulturists.

My grandmother never fretted that her edicts concerning the care of wildlife and maintaining an open door policy to any stranger seeking a meal would go unheeded, because Hilda not only respected her employer's wishes but also shared the same passions. Very little went on in that household that Hilda did not come to know, and any member of the staff caught treating a visitor brusquely or hoarding leftover food would endure Hilda's wrath.

Tears came to my mother's eyes whenever she spoke of Hilda, and she became particularly emotional when she'd tell me how Hilda sheltered my grandparents for a few weeks after *Kristallnacht*. "And at great risk to her own life," my mother would practically shout.

"Not all Germans were Nazis, David," she would say. "Not many at all—not really. Take Hilda, our cook."

"I know, Mother, but Hilda loved your family. To her, you were probably 'good' Jews," I'd say with a smirk. "Did she help other Jews?"

"You don't know what—what you are saying," my mother would say. This sort of talk flustered her, and she would twirl the side curls of her hair with her fingers.

"I think I do, Mother. I think I do."

But it was pointless to argue about it, though we regularly did, since neither of us would ever concede that the other might be just a little bit in the right. As I look back now, I can see that my mother's stubbornness was at least partially rooted in the fact that, as a child, she pretty much had her way.

Like most only children in wealthy families, my mother was spoiled and the center of attention. Her father pampered her just as, a generation later, he indulged me in much the same fashion. She was her maternal grandparents' favorite grandchild, and at family gatherings her cousins glared at her with the jealous scowl of Joseph's brothers envying the wondrous coat of many colors. She was bright, tall, and statuesque, the epitome of the dark-haired Jewess with burning brown eyes. I'm sure she was the object of many a boy's adolescent fantasy and envied by her blond, blue-eyed female classmates at the mostly Gentile school she attended. Did all of this make what happened next even more painful? Perhaps.

When my mother found herself completely alone in a foreign country, with no training to earn a livelihood, I can't imagine how she dealt with the irony of living in a stately home again—as housekeeper rather than mistress. Did this turn of events fill her with bitterness? Of course. Could she reveal even a hint of this resentment to her employers? Absolutely not. For "Madam" and "Sir," as she still referred to the couple whose promise of a job made her entry into the United States possible, deserved her gratitude. She learned to respond with a smile or curtsy or bowed head to the stern doses of discipline they dispensed in training her to become a productive and efficient domestic. The alternative was "Back to Deutschland and see how you like it there!"

Even decades later, my mother would only tell me of these things when I prodded her. As I listened to these stories, I began to understand her extraordinary insecurities. I could not, however, accept what it did to her, how this anxiety formed her life. Her accumulation of precious stones and diamonds, her forgiving my father any transgression—real or imagined—so long as he supplied a new addition to her collection, began to make sense. Jewelry can be transported out of the country easily if one must leave in a hurry and there isn't time to liquidate assets. Other acquisitions, however, I could not fathom.

"Why a Mercedes, Mother?" I asked when she procured her first. "Why a German car? What's wrong with a Caddy or even a Lincoln? After all you and your parents suffered at the hands of the Germans—why a fucking Mercedes?"

But my mother didn't see it that way. She turned a blind eye to the fact that the German government and the German people were the ones who perpetrated the genocide of six million Jews. She remained steadfast in distinguishing "Germans" from "Nazis." Most Germans, she claimed, did not support the Nazi Party. Indeed, my mother assigned more blame to the Slavs, Poles, and Russians for eagerly providing an endless supply of willing accomplices to murder the Jews.

"How can you say such a thing?" I would ask.

"Because they always hated the Jews," my mother would sneer. "For centuries, David—and you know this very well—the Jews were treated far worse by the Russians and Slavs than by the Germans. In Germany, Jews were given the benefit of the Enlightenment while in Russia they were banished to live in the Pale of Settlement, forbidden to live in cities like Moscow."

And there was even more blame to go around as far as my mother was concerned. She condemned the Allies for not making liberation of the death camps a priority. She would not forgive the rest of the world for doing nothing to help save Jews and for not opening their borders. And yet she held Germans (and she still considered herself German) to a less exacting standard.

At the first opportunity, she planned a visit to Germany. Though she wanted to show me off, I refused to go. Decades after escaping the Nazi specter, she returned in all her glory—mink coat, dazzling jewelry, a wealthy American husband, and fancy clothes—to impress those who had once shunned her. She enjoyed it so much that it became an annual pilgrimage to visit, as she said, her old friends.

I was incredulous. "Friends? You call them friends? Where were these 'friends' when you were tossed out of school for being a Jew? How many times did you tell me no one would play with you? And what about being chased and called a *schmutziger Jude*? How can you possibly go back to these people?"

"You don't understand, David," she would say. "There were very few real Nazis. Most of the people were just afraid."

"Oh yeah? If there were so few Nazis in Germany, how did Hitler get elected in the first place? Believe me, Mother, it will be a cold day in hell before I ever set foot on German soil."

"Not even to see our house?"

"Not even that."

I've come to wonder, too, if it was the loss of her childhood home that prompted my mother to keep moving from one house to another—as if in search of the home to which she could never return. Once my father retired, my parents and their snowbird friends began flocking to Florida. My parents bought a condo in Miami Beach overlooking the ocean, which is where I visited them when my conscience got the better of me.

My mother's escape from the Holocaust came with a formidable price tag. She was filled with a fear that whatever was before her would be snatched away. Growing up, I never saw her deriving pleasure from much of anything or becoming unnecessarily attached. Take one day at a time and hope to make it to the end, intact and unscathed—this was her mantra, no matter what the occasion—a party, a bar mitzvah (mine), a birthday, a vacation, a trip, a shopping spree, a movie, an opera, a holiday dinner. She always seemed to want to get through the day so she could safely deposit it in the past, where no one could take it away. Get there, get it done, and scramble back to safety.

As I've searched through photos in the family album, watched movie reels on an antiquated 8mm projector, and delved into memory, I've been unable to summon an image of my mother laughing or smiling. And sadly, until Feig came into my life, I wasn't much different.

But Feig reminded me how grateful I should be that I still had my mother with me and that she had not been taken away prematurely. It was when I was lying on the recliner at the Health Club that day, trying to blink away the vision of Miss Schneider glaring at me over her horn rimmed glasses, that Feig began to tell me the story of what happened to his own mother.

31

"It was sometime late in May, 1944," Feig began as he settled into the reclining chair next to mine. He spoke barely above a whisper, even though there was no one else around to hear him. Just me and Feig.

"My father and I had been working in the Jewish Labor Brigade for several weeks." I nodded. He was continuing his narrative from where he had left off. Although I'd often wondered, I'd never been able to imagine what it must have been like for my grandparents, who were also forced to perform menial tasks to keep the Jewish ghetto going. They'd never spoken about it. I held my breath as he paused. Maybe his account would give me a glimpse into the desperate situation my grandparents survived. Feig went on.

"We were put to work outside Budapest. Conditions were very harsh, you know. We slept on the ground. Nothing over our heads. If it rained, we got wet. If the mosquitoes were ravenous—we were their fodder. The gendarmes fed us two meals a day—gruel in the morning and soup with bits of meat at night. We also were given stale bread that you soaked in the soup to soften it.

"My father had been a burly man with a hearty appetite. In those few weeks, he shrank before my eyes. I didn't change much because I had always been thin and never ate much anyway. But I was hungry then, David. Always, I was hungry." Out of the corner of my eye I saw Feig loll his head in my direction but I stared straight up into the darkness above.

"Sometime late in May, or early June, orders came for us to be marched back to Budapest. We bivouacked by the sidetrack of a great railway yard. I'm not certain what the Hungarian gendarmes had in mind for us and I never did find out," he said. "And you know, David, some of these gendarmes—our fellow Hungarians—were worse than the Germans. They relished beating us and degrading us and even killing us."

I shifted my eyes to sneak a look at him, twisting in his chair to lean my way. "The whole world hates Jews, David. All the *goyim* do—even today." He spat these last words and I thought how my mother would agree. But I didn't agree. The Holocaust was an aberration not likely to be repeated, I wanted to tell him. Anti-Semitism will be with us as long as there are Jews, and we'll be subjected to acts of hatred like all minorities. But a repeat of Auschwitz? I said nothing, however, as I wanted him to go on.

"It was mid-afternoon and unusually hot," Feig continued. His tone was more subdued. "The sun burned in the sky and my skin turned red. Trains had been passing by all day, but then one arrived that I can never forget.

"There were only cattle cars on this train. Barbed wire ran across small openings on the sides. Behind the barbed wire we saw faces—human faces—pressed to the screens. Noses and lips, some gushing blood from being sliced by the wire, protruded like cow snouts sniffing for a whiff of freedom.

"David, I just could not understand what the people were doing in those cattle cars. Nor what could be so terrible inside that drove them to risk gashing their faces for a bit of fresh air and sunshine. Now, of course, I know." He shifted his head in my direction again, and still I stared at the dark ceiling.

"When the transport came to a standstill," Feig said, "the faces began to scream. It was very hot, and it must have been like an inferno inside those cars. We all stopped what we were doing and stared at those wretched souls. What crime could possibly justify this treatment?

"Then I learned the nature of their 'crime.'" I couldn't see his crooked sneer, but I had seen it often enough that I knew his lips were pressed tight and twisted. "Once the shouting became more distinct," he went on, "we realized they were yelling in Yiddish. Their frantic eyes focused on us. They knew we were Jews because of the Star of David on our jackets. And then I knew that my *landsleit*'s only 'crime' was being Jewish.

"They were shouting for water. I was standing near a bucket filled with water, but I was too afraid to do anything. Though I'd only been in the labor brigade a few weeks, I knew that the best way to stay alive was to be invisible. Any move might be enough to prompt a gendarme or Nazi officer to shoot you dead.

"But then I saw the face of a sweet little girl who reminded me of my younger sister. Her eyes pleaded with me. I shall never forget her. She was silent, but I knew what she wanted.

"I filled the ladle in the bucket with water. When the guard closest to me wasn't looking, I darted to the cattle car. By the time I reached her, I had spilled half of the water but she slurped up the rest as I tilted the ladle against the slot. I asked her where she was from. You can imagine my shock when she said, "Sighet."

"I looked at her. Dark eyes in deep sockets. Her black hair matted and her face smudged with soot and who knows what else. And she smelled worse than the shit of cattle or people. I couldn't place the smell then, but I would become familiar with it soon enough.

"I began yelling at the girl, demanding to know if she'd seen my mother and sister but, before she could reply, whoever had been holding her up released her and she disappeared. Other faces took her place. I dropped the ladle and ran to my father, shouting that the train was carrying people from Sighet.

"This was a stupid thing to do, of course, and I attracted the attention of a Hungarian gendarme who plodded toward me. But I didn't care. I only wanted to find my mother and sister. My father grabbed me by the shoulders and demanded to know if what I had said was true. I nodded and my father charged off to the first opening he reached and called for my mother and sister.

"When there was no answer, he bounded to the next car like a man possessed. He ran from one car to the other, howling their names. I tried to keep up but soon fell behind.

"Up ahead, I saw a black-plumed gendarme, couldn't have been more than five or six years older than I was, strut towards my father. He shouted that the "Yid" should tell him what he was up to. When my father ignored him, he became angry, repeated his question, and scowled. My father continued to ignore him, so he smacked the butt of his rifle into my father's back. My father fell to his knees, turned around, and stared past the gendarme at me. I understood his look. I was to remain silent.

"'Why are you so concerned with the *yids* from the countryside?' he shouted. Then he spat into my father's face. My father wiped the spittle from his eyes and said that he was searching for his family. I watched as a thought spread slowly across the gendarme's stupid face. Perhaps the man on the ground was not from Budapest. He demanded to know where my father was from.

"Before my father could answer, the train's whistle blew and the cars lurched forward. My father struggled to his feet and ran after the train, away from the gendarme, screaming for his wife and daughter. The gendarme raised his rifle and fired one shot. It hit my father in the back of the head.

"I ran past the cackling gendarme to my father, who was laying face down. I saw blood and brains oozing from his skull. I kneeled and turned him over so I could look into his face. His eyes were open but he was not looking at me. Not like he used to. His eyes were always smiling … even when he was angry with me. His eyes could never be angry with me, you know. But they were not smiling. They were dead.

"I rocked and cradled my father in my arms—the way he must have held me when I was a baby. And, in a way, it was like I was holding a baby." Feig sighed. He turned his head in my direction once again and, once again, I stared straight ahead and pretended not to notice. He went on. He had to. He had become a prisoner of his own narrative.

"My father had become so light, you know, he seemed to hardly weigh anything. I felt as though I could carry him away in my arms—away from the screeching cattle cars, away from the shouting soldiers, away from Budapest and the labor brigade, away from a world where Jews were brutally man-handled and starved and murdered. I wanted more than anything to carry my father back to Sighet, to rejoin my mother and sister who somehow had never been placed on that train and sent to their deaths. I wanted my father—my father," Feig choked, "to still be alive and I wanted everything to be as it had always been."

I thought I detected a quiet sob, but all I could do was murmur something inaudible—to acknowledge his suffering and pain. But look at him? Say something meaningful? Make an effort to comfort him? That was beyond me then. Now, after all Feig and I have gone through, I would act differently. After a moment he cleared his throat and continued.

"I remained frozen where I was, my father still in my arms as the train began picking up steam. Suddenly, the butt of a rifle slammed into my shoulder. I looked up. Through my tears, I saw the mocking face of the gendarme who had murdered my father. I will never forget his face," he hissed.

"His skin was red like the devil's. He had a boy's blotchy pimples but he was old enough to kill. He snorted like a pig. I hated that face, David. Oh, how I hated that face," he seethed. "I wanted to kill him, but I couldn't move. He demanded to know where I was from. When I didn't answer, he concluded I was not from Budapest and belonged on the train.

"Hoisting me by the collar, he tore me from my father and dragged me to the last car of the train as it was pulling away. He lifted the latch and heaved the door open just wide enough to squeeze me through.

"As the train gathered speed, I stumbled into a sea of bodies. Everything was pitch black. I fell to the floor and people were stepping on me. The stench was hideous. I thought I would be crushed to death." He paused. "If only I had been."

4

That night, after Feig told me about his father's murder and being thrown onto the train to Auschwitz—probably the same train transporting his mother and sister—I had a dream. I first had this dream long ago and it kept recurring, I knew, because something in my unconscious remained unresolved. I called it "the lake dream" and it only left me when Feig did. The dream always began the same way.

I'm treading water in a lake. The lake is murky. I can't see my legs thrashing back and forth. I'm not sure how much longer I can keep it up. I'm afraid I'll go under. There's no shoreline in sight, but I start to swim. I'm not getting anywhere. When I finally stop to catch my breath, I scour the horizon.

At long last I spot a strip of beach. A woman is waving to me and I start swimming toward her. I'm getting closer, but not because of my efforts. It's the land that's moving toward me. I keep my head above water so my eyes can remain fixed on the woman. I fear she'll vanish if I let her out of my sight.

The land is drawing nearer. The woman is beginning to look familiar. It's my mother. But she's not the tiny lady with grayish hair and shoulders stooping from osteoporosis. This is the vibrant woman who raised me. Her hair is jet black. Her posture is erect. Firm breasts fill the cups of the bathing suit she is wearing. Her smile is vivacious and her white teeth glisten. She's waving me on. I move my arms and kick my feet.

But my throat is closing up and I have to stop. I can't swallow. My mouth is parched. The lake is chilly but my skin feels like it's on fire.

My tongue laps at the water but it's salty. Salt water in a lake? It doesn't make sense. But I know I shouldn't drink it. The sky

turns purple. Torrents of rain pummel me. I flip over and float on my
back, opening my mouth as wide as I can, collecting the rain like a
cistern.

My thirst quenched, I resume swimming. I'm getting closer to
my mother, but she slips from my sight as an eerie mist envelops her.
The current grows stronger and I feel weary. My legs and arms ache.
The water swirls around me and I can't keep myself from swallowing
some. I start to gag. Phlegm fills my chest. One more gulp, and I know
I'll go down.

I strike a large wooden object. It's a giant spoon. I hoist
myself up and sprawl on the bowl of the spoon, wheezing as the rain
beats upon my face. I roll onto my stomach and peer into the fog.
Squinting, I can make out a silhouette—it's my mother. She's still
waving me on.

I see dark figures slowly begin to encircle my unsuspecting
mother. They are colossal men standing seven feet tall and wearing
black uniforms. They wear helmets emblazoned with red crosses dripping blood. They inch closer and tighten an invisible noose around
her. "Run!" I want to shout, but I have no voice.

Something drifts by me. It's a man, floating face down. I flip
the body over and see my grandfather's bloated face. I must get away,
I think. I paddle as fast as I can. I hear my mother screaming in the
distance. Her cries pursue me but I close my eyes and pretend not to
hear.

That's where the dream ends. Sometimes the giants'
uniforms are gray or dark blue, and sometimes they're disfig-
ured—barely human behemoths with contorted limbs—but
they're always present, hovering above my mother like vul-
tures over carrion. It's almost always my grandfather floating
by, though once or twice after I met him the face was Feig's.
If the water isn't salty it has a putrid smell like feces and I gag

on it. Sometimes the mammoth spoon is a wooden dipper and I cuddle up inside in the fetal position.

Every time the dream ends, whether it's the middle of the night or the morning, I sit bolt 'upright in bed feeling exhausted, as if I'd completed a workout. I'm always soaked with sweat and my mouth is parched. I pull myself out of bed and plod to the refrigerator, where I gulp from a water bottle.

My mother always pointed out that drinking from this water bottle, which I refill with tap water, is a "filthy" habit. But it's a habit I picked up from Opa, who always kept such a bottle in the refrigerator and drank from it as I do now. But his water was fresh spring water from a waterfall in the park near where we lived.

One of my earliest memories is of Opa leading me by the hand to this small waterfall. It seemed like our own special place, because I never saw another soul there. He would fill a jar, haul it back home, and pour the water into the bottle without spilling a drop. He'd always take a swig and offer the bottle to me to do likewise.

One of my favorite memories of Opa was the game we'd play with his pocket watch. In order for him to remove the watch from his vest, I had to ask for the correct time. "Was zeit is it?" I would inquire in the hodgepodge of German and English we used to converse.

Opa almost always made me repeat myself, pretending he didn't understand. He'd try to look serious, drawing his bushy eyebrows together and curling his thin lips. He'd scratch the stubble of gray whiskers on his chin and shrug his shoulders, feigning bewilderment. But his eyes always gave him away. No matter how hard he tried to look serious, his blue eyes glistened with delight at playing this game. Because

I knew he was teasing, I'd play along and repeat the question until he finally was ready to comply.

Eventually, and with great fanfare, Opa would remove the watch that had accompanied him through his years in Theresienstadt. Though the Nazis had confiscated his gold watch, he'd managed to conceal this tarnished silver watch from them. He'd open the lid, look down, and read me the time. "Zehn minuten past drei o'clock," he might say.

Whenever Opa took out the timepiece, he told me about the gold watch the Nazis had seized. It had been handed down from his grandfather to his father on the occasion of his father's bar mitzvah, who had in turn given it to Opa when he turned thirteen. Opa had hoped to pass on the watch to his own son, but since he had only one daughter it fell to me as his grandson. And because he no longer had the gold watch, he promised to give me the silver watch. But his heart gave out before my bar mitzvah.

I did receive the watch, and I kept it in a drawer for many years. Around the time I met Feig, I had the watch polished and displayed it on my desk. Seeing it there every day inspired me to tell its tale, so I wrote a piece that was published in the local paper.

"That was very moving, David," Feig said as I entered the locker room.

"What was?"

"The article you wrote about your grandfather's watch," he said.

"Oh." I half-smiled. "You're one of the few who read it. Thanks."

Feig was leaving as I was arriving. It was one of those days when he finished earlier than usual and I'd been tied up at the office. As I opened a locker, he slipped a leg through his stiff gray trousers that matched his starched gray shirt—the uniform of a school "engineer." I visualized the clothing of his co-workers—wrinkled, soiled with grease, stained with paint, and spotted with soot. But Feig was the sort of man who took pride in everything he did—and he did everything with the intense concentration of a Zen master.

He was tying his shoes hunched over, body taut. His fingers flicked rapidly and his elbows thrust outwards, decisively, when he tied off the lace.

"Really, David, very touching. Ilse enjoyed it as well."

"How is your wife?" I asked.

He shrugged. A shadow passed over his face. "Ilse would like to meet my famous writer friend, you know. Maybe you can come for dinner one night? Perhaps Friday?"

"I'm afraid not on Fridays. I have a standing dinner with my landlady."

"Then another night? Perhaps Sunday?" I really didn't want to go to dinner at the Feig residence, but I could see he wasn't going to leave before securing a commitment from me. I couldn't say, "Sure, we'll have to get together sometime…" and leave it at that. Still, I tried to squirm out of it.

"Sunday wouldn't it be too much for your wife? I know she's not well."

"Oh, I'll do most of the preparation and cleaning up. Of course, Ilse will have her hand in it and take the credit." His eyes sparkled. Feig's eyes almost never sparkled. I didn't have the heart to snuff out the glow.

"Sunday will be fine," I said.

He beamed as though the prophet Elijah had descended from heaven and agreed to honor his home with a personal visit. Withdrawing a pen and pad from his breast pocket, he carefully printed his address in bold block letters.

"Do you need directions, David?"

I looked at the address and recognized the street. "No problem, Jacob. I live nearby. I look forward to meeting your wife."

The standing meal with my landlady was no lie. I could never have come up with something so off the wall as that. While the occasional Shabbat dinner didn't begin as a weekly event, it eventually became one.

It was hard to avoid Mrs. Moskowitz. I called her Mrs. M., as she preferred. I lived in the second-floor apartment of a duplex, and Mrs. M. occupied the first floor. She was a caricature of the typical Jewish grandmother. She was in her seventies and paraded around, inside and out, in a *shmatte*. Her dyed red hair was almost always in rollers, and her rouge looked like two rubies implanted in her cheekbones. A stout woman, she huffed and puffed whenever she had to climb the stairs—and so she tried to avoid them.

Most of the time, if Mrs. M. wanted me, she'd bellow from the foot of the stairway in her singsong Yiddish accent. I don't think she ever spoke more than a couple of common Yiddish idioms, and I doubt she was ever fluent in the language. "*Davidele*, will you help me with the grocery bags?" Or, "*Davidele*, can you put out the trash for me? I would, but *oy*, my back."

I didn't mind helping her—not even when she hovered over me like a mother hen or when she gazed wistfully at me as if I were a prodigal son. And I certainly had no objection to the food she lavished upon me.

On Friday nights, Mrs. M. traded her usual *shmatte* for a dress good enough to be seen in public. After covering her head with a lace shawl, she would light the candles, spread her fleshy hands over the flickering flames, shut her

eyes, and softly sing the prayer. Then she'd arch her faint eyebrows and throw me a look and I would mutter the Hebrew
words blessing the bread and the wine. I hadn't spoken these
words in years before becoming the "man" of Mrs. M's household.

Then we would feast on matzah ball or cabbage soup,
a roasted chicken or brisket of beef, and always one of her famous specialties like Kreplach or chopped liver. For dessert,
she'd bake an apple or crumb cake and serve hot tea in a glass
with little sugar cubes piled in a dish so she could put a cube
between her teeth while sipping—a custom Eastern European Jews practiced for generations.

I never felt guilty about gorging myself at Mrs. M.'s
table because I knew she was lonely and enjoyed cooking for
someone. In a way, I considered myself to be performing a
mitzvah—a good deed—for this widow whose children resided out of town. Her son lived on the West coast—either in
California or Washington or maybe in one and then the other.
She rarely mentioned him, and I don't think he was ever
married and he definitely had no children. I suspected, by her
moan and frown the rare times she did speak about him, that
he might have been gay. Her daughter lived in New Jersey,
but there must have been some rift between them because
she only visited with her children once or twice a year.

Mrs. M. heard me clomping down the stairs on my
way to Feig's that Sunday evening and stuck her head out the
open door. As usual, her red hair was set in rollers, her face
was heavily rouged, and she was wearing a pink and white
shmatte with fluffy pink slippers on her swollen feet. I asked
how she was and she told me she was fine. I told her I was
heading out but wouldn't be back late. She glanced at the

wrapped box of chocolates I was bringing to Feig and his wife and stood waiting for me to tell her where I was going. But I said nothing further.

The layout of our living quarters created an artificial intimacy because Mrs. M. had her single-family home converted to a duplex after her husband died. We shared a front door, and the stairway leading up to my apartment had once been the staircase from the living room to the bedrooms. So, if I came in late, it wasn't unusual for her to hear me and peek out from behind her door, pretending to be peevish that I had awakened her.

But I had no intention of returning late that night unless dinner proved inedible and I felt the need for a corned beef sandwich, pizza, or Chinese take-out. There were plenty of other choices—Mexican, Indian, Russian, Thai, Vietnamese—but I rarely availed myself of the more exotic cuisine. The section of Philadelphia where I lived—commonly called the "Northeast"—hadn't always had so many dining options. When I was a teenager, the middle-class neighborhood had been predominately Jewish and Irish Catholic and I often travelled in from my affluent suburban community to hang out with friends I had made in the Northeast. But, over the years, most of my Northeast contemporaries moved to more opulent environs. And other ethnic groups seeking to climb a rung up the ladder of the "American Dream" replaced them.

I live in the Northeast because of its proximity to my law practice. Although several of the large Center City law firms were anxious to take advantage of my experience and connections, by the time I'd decided to leave my work as a prosecutor I'd lost my appetite for criminal law. Nor did I want to work late nights compiling fifty or sixty billable hours every week or schmooze clients who would pay hefty retainers. Money meant little to me. I had no family and all I needed were the essentials and a reliable car.

I was leafing through the *Legal Intelligencer* one day over lunch when I noticed an ad for a neighborhood practice seeking a young attorney to ease this lawyer's transition into retirement. Since that day's trial had terminated on a last-minute plea bargain, I took the afternoon off and drove to the address. I hadn't even scheduled an appointment. I think it was the only impulsive thing I'd ever done—though it was not to be the last, since Feig would drive me more than once to act on impulse again.

The storefront was not impressive and yet, as soon as I walked into the law offices of Sol Silverstone, Esquire, I knew it was right. Although the matronly woman seated at the antiquated green metallic desk barely glanced over her horn-rimmed glasses to acknowledge my presence, I felt at home immediately. Behind her was a row of matching metal file cabinets exactly like the ones that had been in my father's real estate office.

The desk and file cabinets are still there, as are Sol Silverstone's walnut desk and his brown vinyl executive chair with its crack down the middle of the seat. The latter bears enduring witness to Sol's corpulent rump and his habit of twisting and squirming during conversations (which were always animated and protracted). I changed very little after Sol retired and sold me the practice for a percentage of fees received over a five-year period. Sometimes I've wondered why it is that I fear the unknown that change represents.

I can still see Sol leaning back in that chair, swiveling in one direction and then the other, wagging his finger at the person on the other end of the phone line or flailing his arms to make a point to the person sitting across from him. Sol practiced law more by persuading and cajoling and convincing than by researching or formulating ingenious legal arguments. This is not my style, but it worked for Sol and allowed him to retire early and move to Florida where, on a golf course outside Boca Raton, Sol dropped dead of a heart attack at the age of sixty-four.

As I drove by my office on the way to dinner at Feig's that Sunday, I thought of Sol and his beaming round face and penchant for a good fight and I smiled. The five years of paying off Sol's estate were nearly over and I'd have a few more dollars to spend, though on what I couldn't say.

The Northeast had been transformed since I was a boy, though it remained as fine and safe a community as one was likely to encounter in a city like Philadelphia. Because most of the homes were reasonably priced and the real estate taxes were low, many Asian and Russian immigrants could afford to live there and intermingle with the blue-collar families residing in enclaves surrounding the Catholic parochial schools. There were a few Hispanic and black families but, for the most part, the students of color at the public high school came by bus from inner-city neighborhoods.

For the likes of Jacob Feig, the Northeast was a natural place to live—among the Russian Jews and the dwindling number of older Jewish residents who were content to live out their years in the homes they had inhabited for over four decades.

Feig lived in a cluster of row houses encircled by major thoroughfares and a bustling commercial district. Almost all Northeast homes were row houses or semi-detached dwellings with two floors, but his was a twin-ranch with one floor and a basement.

I was walking up the path, admiring his well-maintained lawn and white picket fence, when I heard the wail of sirens. An ambulance barreled down the street and pulled in front of my car. A burly black man and short squat Hispanic woman dressed in blue threw open the back doors, removed a stretcher, and darted past me. As they approached the steps to the front door, it flew open and I saw Feig's ashen face.

I knew from his grim look, from the resignation I read on his face, that this was serious. He heaved a sigh as the ambulance attendants dashed into the foyer and he shrugged his shoulders when he saw me. He would accept what fate dished out—as he had done all his life. What else is there to do, I could almost hear him say.

Feig followed the paramedics into the house and I stood in the doorway and listened to the rapid-fire questions and Feig's concise, thoughtful answers. Moments later, I stepped aside to make way for the two paramedics struggling under Ilse Feig's weight. Feig, a step behind, was gently touching his wife's shoulder. Her pallid face was tilted, looking up at her husband.

"I must go with them to the hospital, David. Please excuse me."

"What happened?" I asked.

"Not sure," he answered as I followed him out of the house. "Perhaps a stroke. Ilse has very high blood pressure along with her diabetes. Who knows?"

As the paramedics hoisted her into the back of the ambulance, Feig sighed and turned to me. A solitary tear coalesced in the corner of one eye. "I don't know what I'll do without my Ilse." His lips quivered as he turned away and glanced back at his home. Dusk was descending, and his porch light glowed faintly.

"How will you get to the hospital, Jacob? Do you want me to take you?"

"No. They said I could ride in the ambulance, but then how would I get home? I'll take my car."

"I can pick you up at the hospital," I said. "That way you can go with your wife." He gazed at the ambulance as the attendants slammed the rear doors shut.

"I'm afraid Ilse wouldn't know if I was with her or—or not." The tears welled up in his eyes but did not spill over. "Thank you, David. This is very nice of you to offer but I'll be fine."

I stood helplessly while Feig lumbered over to an old model Buick that had been waxed so well its sheen reflected the streetlight above. He lowered himself into the driver's seat and stuck his head out, forcing a smile, but I could see the tears on his cheeks. The Buick door slammed shut.

The ambulance pulled out into the street, siren blaring, and I watched the rear lights of the Buick merge with the flashing red light atop the ambulance as the two vehicles sped into the night.

In those few minutes since I arrived, the sun had set and night had fallen. Feig had lost loved ones before, and I couldn't imagine how he felt as he faced the prospect of that pain again. I wondered: Is loving someone worth it?

5

I didn't have Feig's phone number, and when I called directory assistance the operator told me it was unlisted. I could have driven to his house to find out how his wife was, but I didn't feel comfortable making an unannounced visit. He was, at the time, only an acquaintance from the Health Club.

I was surprised that Bob, the club manager who knew everything and everyone at the Health Club, hadn't heard anything about the situation. Bob first came to the club as a teenager and worked in exchange for a free membership and the opportunity to become a bodybuilder. A black and white glossy of a twenty-something Bob, flexing his sinewy arms and chest, hung in the office. When I told him what I knew about Feig's wife he expressed concern and asked me to keep him informed.

"I would if I could, Bob, but I have no way of reaching him."

"Can't you call him?"

"I don't have his number," I answered.

Bob gazed at me with the same blank expression he wore when performing his mundane duties at the club. Although he was the manager, Bob's responsibilities included everything from signing up members to mopping the steam room. Neither of us thought of the fact that Feig's phone number must have been part his membership file.

Several weeks passed and then, one night while I was getting dressed in the locker room, he walked in. "Hello, David."

I looked up, surprised that I hadn't heard the familiar snap of his shoes on the linoleum floor. He was shuffling towards me, his face sallow, deep lines crisscrossing his forehead. He slouched as though carrying an unbearable weight but his bright azure eyes met mine.

"How's your wife? I wanted to call you but your phone is unlisted." As I said these words I felt the lameness of my own excuse.

Feig sighed and his eyes glistened. "Very bad, David, very bad." His voice broke.

"I'm sorry to hear that," I said. "Was it a stroke?"

"Yes. There are two kinds of stroke, you know. Ilse suffered a hemorrhagic stroke." Of course he had learned the medical terminology for his wife's condition. He wasn't the sort of person who would allow a doctor to get away with the usual patronizing response: "Your wife had a stroke. I'm sorry." Feig would need to know more. Much more.

"This type of stroke is caused by a cerebral hemorrhage—a bleeding in the brain," he went on. "The doctors are rather certain it was the result of her high blood pressure. If only we could have controlled it. But, medications can only do so much and my Ilse is a stubborn woman. She refused to change her ways or her diet. 'Why live if you can't eat?' she used to say. A stubborn woman. Very stubborn." He shook his head.

"Some people are like that," I mumbled. I knew he needed to talk and that it didn't matter what I did or didn't say.

"Now, if we could have gotten her to the hospital sooner," he said. He stared into the distance and then back at me. "Ilse had been unconscious for maybe an hour before I found her. It was the evening you were coming to dinner, David."

Had he forgotten I was at his house that night, standing by the doorway while the paramedics carried Ilse out to the ambulance?

"I was busy in the kitchen and Ilse went for a nap," he continued. "She wanted to be well rested so she could be a good hostess. When I went to check on her to make sure she was up and getting dressed, she was still in bed. I tried to wake her, but she didn't wake up." Feig looked down at the floor. "I should have checked on her before that."

"It's not your fault. You can't blame yourself. You had no way of knowing."

He sighed again. "Yes, I know. In my head, I know this but my heart says otherwise. With a stroke, time is critical. A better chance for recovery."

"What's her prognosis?"

He pulled up a chair and sat down. "No recovery. They perform a test at the hospital, you know, for stroke victims and they score them. The lower the number the better. Single digits are good—especially under seven. Double digits—not so good."

"How did your wife score?"

"Sixteen. It means recovery is not likely and death—" he paused and looked over my shoulder. "Death is just a matter of time."

"I'm sorry," I said. "But doctors don't know everything. That's why they call it the 'practice' of medicine." I knew my words sounded hollow. "Where is she now?"

"In the rehabilitation unit of the hospital. But they will be discharging her in a day or two. The insurance only covers her stay as long as progress can be made. And they say there is no further progress possible."

"Where will she go?"

"Home."

"Can you handle her care?"

"I'm not sure. She's completely paralyzed on one side. She cannot move her arms or legs. She cannot speak and they say she never will. We're not sure whether she can even see or hear or what, if anything, she is thinking. My Ilse is a prisoner trapped within a broken body."

"I don't see how you can care for her, Jacob."

"What choice do I have, my friend?" That was the first time Feig called me his friend. I hadn't thought of myself as his friend. Nor did I consider him to be my friend. But I hadn't thought about it at all, really, though in the weeks and months that followed I would give it a great deal of thought.

Feig continued, answering his own question. "We have no insurance for extended care. I do not have the funds to pay for anything more than the bottom rung of nursing homes. Ilse's children can contribute a little—maybe to help me get some part-time help so I can still work. And her daughter, who lives nearby, said she will help care for her mother. As I said, what choice have I?"

He bared his teeth, and his sardonic smile unnerved me. There was something he wasn't saying. He would never resign himself to a situation in which he had no choice. He would insist on options. There had to be an "either-or" and not just a "take it or leave it." Feig survived by making sure there was a choice he could make.

Before I left, Feig removed a pad and pen from his breast pocket and wrote down his phone number in the same bold block style he had used to inscribe his address a few weeks earlier. This way, he told me, we could stay in touch despite his sporadic attendance at the Health Club.

On my way out of the locker room, I glanced over my shoulder. Feig was slouched over his gym bag, slowly removing his worn sneakers. What puzzled me was that he looked like a man beaten—and yet I knew that he could never be beaten, by fate or by the gods. Feig would decide if and when to accept defeat.

In the weeks that followed, I saw him only once. As I walked by the steam room I saw his slumped body, elbows resting on knees. Without raising his head, he flung the sweat from his brow. I opened the door and asked how his wife was. She was the same, he said. I asked how he was managing. He shrugged and said that he was managing. I asked if there was anything I could do to help, and he thanked me but said there was nothing anyone could do. Before the hot wet air could soak my gym clothes, I said goodbye. By the time I finished my workout, Feig was gone.

A few more weeks passed. I called him once and left a message asking if I could pick up take-out food and drop off a dinner. He left a message on my machine, saying that he appreciated the offer but he was getting by. We had no further contact until one evening several weeks later.

I didn't get to the Health Club until well past seven that night due to a protracted real estate closing. What should have taken one hour took three, and by the time I arrived at the club I was exhausted. After pushing myself through a workout followed by a steam, I collapsed into an easy chair and fell asleep.

Suddenly there was a tugging at my elbow and I awoke, not knowing where I was or what time it was. Bob was hovering above me. "Are you awake? Are you awake?" he was asking.

I grumbled.

"Are you awake? Are you awake?"

"Christ, Bob! What does it look like? If I wasn't awake, I am now!"

Bob stood back and stared at me, wide-eyed.

"All right," I said as I regained consciousness. "What do you want?"

"There's a phone call for you."

"Couldn't you take a message?"

"It's Mr. Feig. He says he must speak with you and that it is important."

"OK. Tell him I'll be right there," I said. "Thanks." I felt guilty that I had yelled. Bob scurried down the corridor to the public phone affixed to the wall. Bob didn't permit members to use the office phone, and if there was a personal call for someone he always made whoever it was call back on the public phone. I pressed my calves down, returning the recliner to the upright position, and wrapped a towel around my waist. The receiver was swaying to and fro where Bob had dropped it. "Hello."

"David? Is this you?"

"Yes. What is it, Jacob? Is everything OK?"

A long pause followed before Feig answered. "David, Ilse is dead."

"When?"

"This morning."

I was surprised that I was on his list of people to call and I wondered why he didn't leave a message on my machine. Since her death was not a shock, I was fairly composed in offering my condolences. I even tried to assuage his pain and rationalize his loss.

"I'm sorry, Jacob. But you said she was suffering. Now she won't suffer any longer. Maybe it's better."

"Oh yes, no doubt. Listen, David," I had trouble hearing him over his heavy breathing. "This is the thing. There are some questions." He hesitated again.

"What do you mean questions? About what? Her will? Is there a will? If not, then—"

"No. Not that. There are questions, you know, about her death."

"No. I don't know," I said.

"There is to be an autopsy, David."

"Why?"

"The circumstances of her death."

"What are you talking about, Jacob? What's going on?"

"David, can you come here?" Feig knew his house was practically on my way home from the club. Given the late hour I had no excuse to offer, so I hardly had a choice. I confirmed the address and said I would see him in half an hour.

The weariness of the day was returning. I wanted to get dressed and go home, maybe defrost a pizza or nuke Mrs. M.'s leftover brisket. Instead, I plodded back down the hallway to the locker room and dressed. On my way out of the club, I stopped by the office to let Bob know about Feig's wife. But he was on the phone and didn't look up, so I left.

Even if I hadn't been there before, I would have known Feig's house. In the Jewish religion, funerals take place within a day or two of death, absent a holiday or Shabbat. The mourning period begins after the burial and, if strict observance is followed, the immediate family should be left alone until that time. But usually this is not the practice, and close friends and family members often visit before the funeral.

Feig's house, ablaze with lights, stood out like a lighthouse in a sea of darkness. As I walked towards the house I watched the shadowy figures pantomime behind the curtains. I didn't ring the bell or knock. Another Jewish custom is to leave the door unlocked so visitors can walk in and not disturb the mourners. I entered and found myself in the living room among a dozen or so people.

Naturally, I didn't recognize any of them. Feig was nowhere in sight. A middle-aged woman on the sofa was dabbing a handkerchief at the mascara running down her cheeks. A balding man was seated beside her, his head tilted and his fleshy hands folded on his lap. He was squinting at me as if trying to determine if he knew me from somewhere.

This pair shared a certain roundness to their shoulders, high foreheads, beefy necks, brown hair, and thin lips. I suspected they were Ilse's children. Also seated on the sofa was a gaunt man with an arm around the woman whom I took to be his wife. Several teenagers were eating sandwiches from paper plates and the rest of the people were milling around and talking. Every so often, one of them would step over to the sofa to say a few words or touch the leg or shoulder of one of the mourners.

I hung in the doorway, shifting from foot to foot. Finally Feig appeared, carrying a coffee percolator. He set it down on the dining room table. When he spotted me, he arched his bushy eyebrows and sidled in my direction. As he made his way through the group, I observed something odd. The people swayed, stepped back, twisted, and turned to avoid physical contact with him. The vacant gaze of the man on the sofa followed Feig as he passed by. For a split second something sinister replaced that empty look, but then it vanished and the void returned.

"Thank you for coming, my friend." Feig grasped my hand with both of his.

"I'm sorry for your loss, Jacob." He held tight to my hand. I glanced over at the sofa. "Are they your wife's children?" I asked.

He didn't look in their direction. "Yes, Ilse's son and daughter." With a nod toward the three teenagers huddled in the corner with their sandwiches, he added, "And those are Ilse's grandchildren. Ilse loved them dearly. They even called her *bubbe*. Isn't that something for American teenagers to do?" He sighed. "Come with me, my friend, where we can talk."

Feig released my hand in order to take my elbow and lead me toward the kitchen. The people standing in the living room and around the dining room table made way for us as I imagined the Sea of Reeds must have parted for Moses leading the Hebrews. Or, more likely, as people avoided a leper whose slightest touch might infect them.

"Oh David, forgive me. Is there something you would like to eat or drink?" I'd missed dinner and was hungry but, not wanting to prolong my stay, I took a cold soda and followed him down the stairs into the basement. Part of the cellar was partitioned into a finished room with a tile floor and paneled walls. I sat on a small sofa and Feig settled into an armchair. He leaned over. His jagged face was so close that I looked at the gray stubble of his budding beard and scratched my own chin.

"They want to do this autopsy, you know."

"Yes. You told me. But why?"

Feig sighed and rolled his eyes upward, as if he could see through the ceiling and into the living room. "It's Marsha, Ilse's daughter. And her brother. They and that quack of a doctor who they call the 'family physician.' They think something is not right."

"What do you mean?" I asked. I was beginning to get the picture, though. I'd dealt with enough wills and estates to hear a lot of grumbling about who gets what, and especially in cases where there's been a second marriage. I knew it was impossible to underestimate the depths of human avarice and the demons it arouses. "Does Ilse have a will?"

"That's not the thing." He shooed my comment away with his hand. "David, they think I killed Ilse." He spoke barely above a whisper and I wasn't certain I'd heard him correctly.

"They think what?"

"That I killed Ilse."

"That's crazy," I said.

Feig remained silent. He withdrew into the corner of the armchair and rested his chin on his fist. His eyes deepened to a murky bluish hue as he stared into me.

A chill ran through my bones.

6

I sat across from Feig in the basement room, shocked and waiting for him to say more. How was it possible that he stood accused of murdering his wife? He described the stormy scene that occurred barely an hour after he found Ilse dead and dialed 911.

"As soon as they arrived, Ilse's son and daughter accused me of killing their mother, David. They blockaded the doorway to the room where their mother lay."

"What did you do?" I asked.

"I told them it was my bedroom and my wife lying in our bed and they had no right. No right. I told them they should be ashamed of themselves. I told them their mother would be appalled." He looked off into the distance.

"What did they say?"

"Norma said that I killed her, that her mother was fine and not anywhere near death. I told her she was crazy. 'Your mother could not move, speak, or eat,' I reminded them. Norma had spent enough time feeding her mother through a plastic straw to know that saying she was 'fine' was utter nonsense!"

But, Feig said, there was no convincing Norma or her brother Mark. "They cajoled and threatened and persisted until Dr. Emile Firestein, that quack doctor, agreed to examine Ilse more thoroughly. He didn't find anything unusual but they got him to agree to request an autopsy."

Norma and Mark's accusation had nothing to do with pecuniary considerations. Feig stood to gain almost nothing by his wife's death. Ilse had left her entire estate, what there was of it, to her children and grandchildren. The only provision for Feig was a "life interest" in the home they had occupied together. In other words, he was permitted to remain in the house for the rest of his life as long as he paid the real estate taxes and maintained the property. That wasn't much motivation to murder someone, and Ilse's children knew this. They were aware of the terms of their mother's will. So what was it that made them suspect Feig had killed their mother?

Looking back, I suppose I should have known. Jacob Feig was a Holocaust survivor and he had witnessed suffering and anguish others cannot imagine in their darkest nightmares. The grief of a parent helplessly watching a child starve to death. A mother leading her daughter by the hand down a bleak corridor into a room packed with naked bodies awaiting death to pour from shower heads. A husband gazing beyond the pale of barbed wire surrounding a desolate gray building where his wife is fucked by forty men a day—for which he must be grateful, since otherwise she'd be ashes spewing from a chimney into the black sky. A thirteen-year-old boy cradling the body of his dead father, shot before his eyes, blood and brains oozing from his head.

Feig understood pain in the very marrow of his being. And, because of this, decades earlier—in another lifetime, in another world—he had resolved that he would never allow someone he loved to suffer.

Which is why I should have known. Which is why Ilse's children were suspicious. Dr. Emile Firestein suggested, and the coroner confirmed, that the cause of Ilse Feig's death was an overdose of Gabapentin, prescribed for pain, and the antidepressant Paxil. The coroner's conclusion was unambiguous: someone had crushed all of the pills from the newly-filled prescriptions into a liquid solution and given the deadly potion to Ilse through a straw, which was retrieved from the scene by the police. It took no great leap of imagination to conclude that the person who placed the lethal straw through Ilse's lips was her husband, Jacob Feig.

Should I have seen this coming? In the early morning hours, after Feig was roused from his bed in the middle of the night and handcuffed, my phone rang. Only when I heard his quaking yet controlled voice, asking that I represent him and then demanding that I make certain he was liberated at once, did Feig's arrest seem real to me. I had never acknowledged anything unpleasant unless I had no other choice. I had always lived that way and had no plan to do otherwise. But that would soon change, and I would never be the same.

My connection with Jacob Feig was responsible for another dramatic turn in my life. For Feig, indirectly, reconnected me with Carol Silverberg. More than a decade had passed since I'd seen her—when I was still an assistant district attorney and she had recently been admitted to the Bar. Our paths had first crossed a few years before that at Penn Law School, when I was in my third year and Carol was beginning her first.

The first time I spied Carol, she was striding through the two-hundred-year-old archway leading into the lobby of the law school building. Her green eyes brimmed with confidence as she crossed the threshold, as if she were about to conquer the world. As I watched her, I remembered how tentative my first steps into this ivy-covered stone building with its marble floor and centuries of heritage had been. This stunning young woman tossed her long auburn hair and gazed up at the spiral granite stairway where I stood, transfixed.

When her eyes met mine, it was all I could do not to avert my gaze in embarrassment. The sensitivity I saw in her verdant and sparkling eyes seemed to invite me in—and yet that invitation was qualified. She strode up the staircase, smiling as she approached, and I smiled in return. I was about to say hello when the sunlight through the glass dome above struck the diamond on her ring finger and blinded me with its glare. My eyes adjusted and settled on the glittering gem as she passed and I said nothing.

Weeks later, I saw her in the library. She was flitting from one shelf to another, her delicate fingers trailing along the numbered volumes to locate the right tomes. Though I could tell from her drawn brow and set chin that she knew exactly what she was doing, I decided this was the opportunity I'd been waiting for and offered to help.

Carol was preparing her first memorandum of law, she said, and she was sure she could find what she would need. But, I pointed out with a glint in my eye, it would take so much less time if I helped. She giggled, and my insides glowed from the warmth of her smile. She agreed, but only if she could buy me a cup of coffee in return.

Thus our friendship began. I could hardly have expected more than friendship. Carol was engaged. Should she have considered breaking her engagement because of me? Because of the innuendoes I coyly dropped from time to time? The slight touch of my hand upon hers? My grasping her elbow as I led her through the library's stacks? The way I gazed at her like some starry-eyed adolescent?

But I did not give her the slightest intimation that I was falling in love with her. If I declared myself, I thought, would I be prepared to vie with a man who sounded like a decent enough fellow? Would I lose Carol and her friendship? Or, if I prevailed and she left her fiancé for me, could I commit to a long-term relationship? I didn't know if I was ready for that.

So I assumed the role of Carol's mentor during her first year of law school. I concealed my deepest feelings when we were together. Only at night, unable to sleep, did I allow my growing ardor free rein as I fantasized about what I might do or say to her the next day. But, when the next day arrived, I neither said nor did anything of the kind.

After I graduated and began my stint as a prosecutor, we lost touch. When I read her marriage announcement in the paper, I thought of calling and offering my congratulations. But I kept putting it off until, many months later, it was too late for such a call. And then I met Eve.

After I graduated from law school, my mother began to nag me in earnest about my looming bachelorhood. She never said anything directly, but her message was clear. Oma and Opa did not survive the Holocaust, nor did she, to see the family line end with a capricious progeny.

"David, I have someone for you to call," my mother would say. She'd describe a nice Jewish girl, usually in her senior year of college and planning to be a teacher, who would make a wonderful wife and mother. I'd listen, knowing that any objection would only prolong the conversation. I'd dutifully take the phone number and promptly misplace it. In this way I managed to avoid at least a dozen candidates before meeting Eve. There was no way to avoid that introduction—my mother bushwhacked me at the synagogue.

By that time I no longer attended synagogue. I had given up on a god to whom people were to address prayers. I found the notion of an anthropomorphic deity, patiently fielding mortal supplications and thoughtfully responding, to be absurd and puerile. So why pray? And since synagogues, like churches and mosques, are essentially places of prayer, why go? But when my father had to work the night of a synagogue-sponsored evening for Holocaust survivors, I agreed to accompany my mother. That was when I met Eve.

Eve. Even now, so many years later, I'm not sure which of the labels from the DSM correctly applied to her. Whether she suffered from bipolar disorder, manic depression, schizophrenia, obsessive-compulsive disorder, or paranoia depended on which shrink was treating her. She tried an array of therapies and medications, from electroshock to group to analytic psychotherapy to just about every pill in the pre-Prozac psychiatric arsenal. She endured several inpatient stints at mental facilities and, so she claimed, made more than one attempt at ending her life. And all this before she was twenty-two.

But I knew nothing of her troubles when my mother, who was also in the dark about Eve's demons, expertly orchestrated the introduction. A woman who had been a "hidden child" in France during the War was speaking at the synagogue that evening. Raised a Catholic, this woman did not learn of her Jewish roots until after the War had ended. She had written a book about her experience, and this book was one of the first I reviewed for the local Jewish tabloid.

After the presentation, everyone congregated over coffee and cookies. I was walking across the room to talk with the speaker when I felt a familiar tug on my elbow.

"David, there's someone I want to meet." The pale, slender woman standing next to my mother reminded me of a newborn bird, bopping about in the nest with its beak gaping in a frenzy waiting for something—anything—to fill it. Her brown eyes darted about while she nervously shifted from one foot to the other. But I was stuck with my back pinned, literally, against the wall.

We politely exchanged greetings, and the corners of Eve's mouth turned upward in a tightlipped, nervous smile. She was pretty, with jet-black hair, but I'm not sure I would have taken a second look if she'd been walking down the street. The instant we shook hands, though, something happened. The touch of her fingertips delicately scraping the inside of my palm sent a shiver of excitement through my body. I didn't want to let go, and only when it became painfully awkward did I release my grip and allow her to withdraw her hand—but not before she scratched her fingernails across my wrist. I was ensnared the way a bee is drawn to a flower. Perhaps I should have seen that a better metaphor might have been a mouse lured by the scent of cheese set in a trap ready to snap.

"I knew Eve's father," my mother said. She was beaming at the obvious attraction she saw between us. I could see her thoughts racing to plan the wedding and reserve the date with the rabbi. "Eve's father lived near our home in Germany, David," my mother continued. "He was a friend of Oma's youngest brother, Daniel. Such a handsome man! I was barely a teenager and had a crush on him." Eve and my mother exchanged girlish giggles.

"But then came the War. Your father was married by then, wasn't he, Eve?" Eve nodded. "He also had a little girl, if I remember," my mother added. Eve nodded again.

"They were in Theresienstadt with Oma and Opa. But they were sent to Auschwitz and only Eve's father survived." My mother sighed as she always did when speaking of someone killed in the Holocaust. "Imagine, David, after all those years, Eve's father and I crossed paths at the German synagogue where Oma and Opa belonged. Remember, David? I took you there once."

"Vaguely, I was just a kid," I said. My eyes had not left Eve's.

"Well, by that time Eve's father was remarried and I met his wife and cute little daughter." My mother smiled at her. "Your father died. Was it six years ago?" Eve lowered her eyes. "But Eve's mother and I keep in touch. Your father and I visit her when we're in Florida."

And that was it. If my mother could have seen what lay ahead, she'd have torn Eve away from me and made certain that we never saw each other again.

At first, I attributed Eve's volatile behavior to smoking pot and occasionally snorting coke, which was not an uncommon practice in the seventies. But eventually I discovered that, though the pot and coke certainly didn't help, they were not the cause of her violent mood swings.

What held us together for more than a few years was our mutual physical desire. Sex was the keystone of our relationship. It bound us to each other when we should have come undone. While we sometimes used the word "love" in the throes of passion, I don't believe we ever loved each other—even if at times Eve might have thought otherwise.

Eve and I dated exclusively because she would have it no other way. I resisted the idea at first but soon realized I had no choice—unless I wanted to endure the turbulent tantrums that erupted whenever she suspected I had other romantic interests. I learned this the hard way about a year into our relationship.

On her way to paying me a surprise visit at the District Attorney's Office, Eve spotted me in a restaurant having lunch with Carol, who was doing an internship in the Public Defender's Office. Carol had called me to ask how best to approach another assistant DA on a case and we had agreed to meet for lunch.

Carol and I were just starting our salads when a shrill cry, like that of a wounded animal, shattered the tranquil ambiance of the room.

"David! You fuck!"

All eyes but mine turned to Eve. Like an ostrich burying its head, I decided that if I didn't see the twisted, screaming figure storming in our direction, it would leave me alone.

"You son-of-a-bitch! What about our lunch date?"

"What lunch date?" I stammered. "We have no lunch date."

"It was going to be a surprise," Eve said. She put her hands on her hips like an indulgent teacher explaining the answer to the pop-quiz question of the day.

I knew that anything I said would inflame rather than calm Eve, who was glaring at Carol. Carol was leaning away from Eve, her eyes wide and her mouth agape. I stood and stepped toward Eve.

But Eve bolted, knocking over a server carrying a tray of drinks on her way out of the restaurant. I didn't even try to follow her but returned, red-faced, and concocted a story for Carol. I'd prosecuted a case against Eve's abusive boyfriend, I explained, but she wasn't satisfied with the sentence he received. To keep her from causing a ruckus in the courtroom and being hauled off to jail herself, I told Carol, I'd muttered something about discussing the matter with her over lunch.

"The poor deranged woman must have decided we'd meet for that lunch today," I concluded.

I could tell from the furrows in her brow that she didn't buy it, but she graciously accepted my explanation. Our conversation was strained, and we soon parted. We wouldn't see each other again for over a decade—until Feig caused our paths to cross again.

A slew of messages on my answering machine greeted me that evening. "You prick! Who was that slut with you, David?" That was Eve's first message. Then a hang-up followed by a series of curses and more hang-ups. The final message was almost incoherent. "I love you, David," she sobbed. "How could you do this to me? I can't live without you." I called back. No answer. She had attempted suicide before, or so she said. I ran down the stairs and drove to her apartment.

I found Eve slumped in the center of her bed and clad only in a loose tee shirt. Her long raven hair fell forward so I couldn't see her face or if she was breathing or if there was blood anywhere. Then I heard a snort and her head shot back. She lifted her face and smiled. Some of the white powder was still on her nostrils.

"Christ, Eve! Why the hell do you take that shit?"

"Makes me feel good, David. Makes me feel alive," she cooed. And, before I could vent my anger, Eve had crawled across the bed, grabbed my crotch, unzipped my fly, and brought me to my first orgasm of the evening.

Eve hadn't killed herself, nor had she ever intended to. I resolved never to let her have that kind of hold over me again. I wouldn't run to her again like some stupid puppet on a string—though, I have to confess, I was glad I came that night.

It wasn't until shortly before our relationship ended that I learned the cause of Eve's psychological and emotional problems—although I'm still not sure she told me the truth. For she was an expert at fabricating lies and perceiving reality in a wholly different way than most of us do.

Eve blurted out her "deep dark secret," as she referred to it, the evening of my thirtieth birthday. We had reservations at a special restaurant to mark the occasion. When I arrived to pick her up, she wasn't waiting outside as she usually did. I took the stairs to her apartment and let myself in the unlocked door. She was in the living room, sprawled on the sofa in a daze.

"Eve! Aren't you ready? You look horrible," I said. I made no effort to conceal my annoyance. She was dressed in jeans and a red halter-top. Her hair was frazzled. She gazed at me through bleary eyes.

"Ready for what?" she murmured.

"My birthday dinner! That's what!"

"Oh, I'm sorry, David. Is it tonight?"

"Yes, it's tonight. Christ, Eve. I blew off my parents and said I'd see them tomorrow so we could be together tonight." I chose not to add that neither of my parents were pleased that I was spending my birthday with her. Even though my mother had introduced us, it hadn't taken her long to begin to regret it.

"I'm really sorry, David," she cooed. She began slinking along the sofa like a cat on the prowl and gestured for me to sit next to her. "I had a very bad night and couldn't sleep. Just dozed off this afternoon." She stretched her arms and yawned. But her charms didn't have their desired effect. I was pissed.

"Well, you should have called me," I said. "How could you forget my birthday dinner? You practically planned the damned thing!" She had selected the restaurant and made the reservation, which was about as much as she was capable of planning.

"I had something else on my mind, David." The tone she used to enunciate my name was a sign she was shifting gears. I knew I was in for a firefight. We never argued much because I usually backed off. But I was in no mood for letting up that night.

"And what, pray tell, was so much more important? Your 'career' as an office temp? You have no kids, no responsibilities, and I sure as hell don't make any demands of you! So what is it, Eve? Saving humanity? Cleaning up the environment? World peace?"

She blanched, but only for an instant. Her pale face turned crimson and she spewed forth her retort like cannon fire. "You want to know, David? Fine. I'll tell you. I've kept it in long enough and never let on even once in the fucking four years we've been fucking each other! It's just that, every so often, I get a bit upset from this picture that keeps popping into my head of me being fucked by my daddy. That's what's on my mind!"

"Your father? You're only telling me this now? When did this happen?"

"When I started to grow titties, David!" she hissed. "He began porking me when I was twelve and didn't let up until the day he died. Care to know how my daddy croaked, David dear?" She let out a spine-tingling cackle. "The fucker gave up the ghost in the saddle. He crapped out with his dick in my cunt!"

"Did you?" I couldn't bring myself to ask the question—if Eve had murdered her own father while he was having sex with her.

"No. I didn't kill the bastard, if that's what you're thinking—though I should have. It was an embolism. Daddy never knew what hit him. It was the night before my sweet sixteen party. Some sweet sixteen!" Eve snarled.

I was speechless. The fine gentleman my mother had described had sexually molested his own daughter? But then I thought of what her father must have endured in the Holocaust. In Auschwitz. Losing his wife and child. And who knows what else. Who knows what wounds had festered inside this seemingly well-adjusted man and how they might have manifested themselves in unimaginable ways.

But what upset me most was that I'd never had an inkling about it. She rarely spoke of her father, and I knew that she and her mother didn't get along. She hadn't seen her mother in two years and only seldom made the long-distance call to Florida, where her mother had moved with her new husband. I'd tried more than a few child molestation cases in the District Attorney's Office and knew that blaming the parent who did nothing to prevent the abuse was fairly common.

Should I have tried harder to help her, to find the source of her troubles? I realize now that my relationship with Eve was yet another situation in which I kept myself at a safe distance, my gaze averted from the abomination skulking in the shadows.

But Eve had chosen not to share her secret with me. The years of her silence did lead me to wonder whether her accusation was true. Though it would be like her to make something up for dramatic effect, I couldn't imagine she would fabricate such a lie. I didn't know.

We ended up celebrating my birthday at the restaurant as planned that evening, almost on time, but something had changed. While neither of us brought up the subject again, it lingered—at least for me. Regardless of the face she presented, every time I looked at Eve I saw something odious slinking beneath her skin. Her eyes had lost their seductive glitter and her smirk no longer appeared childlike or impish.

I began making excuses not to see her. Too busy at work. My parents needed me to run errands and help them fix things up around the house. Too tired. Not feeling well—a cold, a virus, a bad headache. At first she threw tantrums and screamed or left nasty messages but, after a few weeks, she seemed resigned that we were drifting apart.

We saw each other occasionally because I couldn't bring myself to break it off completely. But when a week went by and I hadn't heard from her and she didn't answer her phone, I drove to her apartment. Her first-floor neighbor told me that "the wacky girl from upstairs" was dead. Something about drugs. I never knew whether the overdose was accidental or not, but I felt responsible.

Even though I hadn't loved Eve, I mourned her. She said cruel things during her outbursts, but she was also a kind person. I missed her playfulness. I missed having someone who was always available at a moment's notice. And, of course, I missed the sex.

For ten years after Eve's death I lived life at a distance. I began to date again, but only occasionally. At work I was courteous, civil, and sometimes friendly. Sometimes at the Health Club someone would spill his guts—and I would listen, but I kept everything to myself. And then I met Feig.

After Feig called me that morning from jail, I called the Assistant District Attorney assigned to his case—Carol Silverberg. My heart beat wildly as I waited to hear her voice.

"This is Carol Silverberg."

My lips quivered, but I couldn't speak.

"Hello? Who is this?"

"Me." It was all I could muster.

"Who?" I detected her growing impatience in the voice. I had to pull myself together.

"The voice doesn't ring a bell? You don't know who this is?"

"I … I'm not sure."

I was sure she recognized me. I was sure she didn't want to say, "Oh, David! It's you!" and then find out it wasn't.

"It's David Gold."

"David! How are you?" She sounded pleased. She was never good at concealing her feelings and she couldn't tell a lie—which was a hindrance in the practice of law.

"I'm fine. It's been a long time." I was hoping she had forgotten our last meeting.

"It's been too long!"

"I see you're off the hyphenated name and back to 'Silverberg.' Is it easier that way?"

There was a pause. "I dropped the hyphen when I dropped my husband."

My heart pounded and I felt like I did when I asked this cute blond girl out for a date in the seventh grade and she accepted.

"But that's only professionally," Carol continued. "Otherwise, I still use the hyphenated name so it sounds like I'm related to my kids." She laughed. I always loved her childlike giggle.

"I didn't know you were divorced. I'm sorry to hear that. How old are your children?"

"Bobby is eight and Melissa's five."

"That's amazing! I can't believe it's been ten years." Why did I say that? Before Carol could comment on our disastrous lunch, I changed the subject. "So, why the DA's Office?"

"The job fits my needs."

"You have to work?"

"It helps. And the kids are both in school and I'm not the stay-at-home sort."

"I thought you were. I thought that's why what's-his-name married you."

"That's what what's-his-name thought, too, and what's-his-name was wrong." She laughed again.

"What is what's-his-name's name, anyway?" I asked. We both laughed.

Carol changed the subject. "The other thing is that working in the District Attorney's Office is more of a nine-to-five job. And I negotiated to have the summers off so I can have time with my kids."

"Sounds good," I said.

"You know, David, I've thought about you a lot."

I tried to conceal my surprise. "You have?"

"Yes. That first year in law school when you were a mentor to me really meant a lot. It had a huge effect on me and the type of person—not just the type of lawyer—that I've become."

"Really? How?"

"Oh, I can't tell you all that over the phone. Maybe over lunch sometime? But tell me, David, why did you call? Just to chat?"

"Actually, it's about one of your cases—Jacob Feig."

"I didn't know you practiced criminal law."

"I don't very much, but here and there, you know." I glanced around my Spartan office, a space I had decorated to avoid any appearance of opulence. "In a neighborhood law practice you see just about everything. Nothing big, though."

"I wouldn't call a murder case small potatoes."

"Well, it's not your typical murder case. In fact, it shouldn't be treated as a murder at all."

"That's what they all say, David."

"Really, Carol. At most, it's aiding suicide."

"No, David, at best it's a mercy killing, and that means murder—not just criminal homicide."

I was crestfallen that, after such a long time, my first contact with Carol had deteriorated to a sparring match between opposing attorneys. But I had a client to defend and, somehow, I had to separate the personal from the professional.

"Could we put that issue aside for now? I'm calling to ask you not to oppose release on recognizance at the arraignment tomorrow."

"You've got to be kidding."

"I'm not. Look, Carol, I've known this man for some time. I've seen how he dealt with his wife's illness and how much he loved her. And what you don't know is that he's a Holocaust survivor. The fact that he's behind bars is unconscionable. The last time he was incarcerated was at a place called Auschwitz."

"So let him post bail."

"He doesn't have the money."

"Then have him put up the house."

"He doesn't own the house."

"Then you have a problem, David."

I didn't need her to tell me that. There was no way anyone—even an old, broken man like Feig who was unlikely to go anywhere—would be released on his own recognizance with a murder charge. But I was hoping that Carol wouldn't oppose the judge setting a small amount for bail that I could afford to post on Feig's behalf. "Well, how about a nominal amount?" I asked.

"We'll see." I could tell I was making some headway.

"OK, then. Thanks. See you tomorrow."

"Yes, tomorrow."

"I wish it was under better circumstances, Carol."

"Lunch would have been preferable, David. But then again, if not for this, would you have called me?"

Probably not, I thought to myself.

7

"The Roundhouse," as the circular Police Administration Building is commonly called, nestles between the Benjamin Franklin Bridge and Chinatown. Depending on the direction of the wind, people entering the building experience either a delightful aroma of garlic and spices wafting from a multitude of Asian restaurants or the stench of rotting garbage from overflowing cans in the alleyways. On the morning of Feig's arraignment, the reek of rubbish assaulted me.

Directly across from the Roundhouse, a labyrinth of cardboard boxes on a plot of ground provide shelter for those without. It was a perfect site for the homeless. On one side of the lot, six lanes of traffic frequently backed up the ramps leading onto the bridge's narrow expanse, which gave the more enterprising street people the chance to sell trinkets and flowers, wash and wipe windshields, or just plain panhandle. Drivers with their stomachs full of lo mein, chop suey, or General Tso's chicken not infrequently parted with their leftovers. And on the coldest nights, shunning the dangers of the city's shelters where one was just as likely to be robbed or beaten as to get a decent night's sleep, many vagrants would loiter on the steps of the Roundhouse hoping to be arrested and spend the night in a warm bed safe behind bars.

After years of serving as the doormat to the tens of thousands sucked into the swamp we call a criminal justice system, the Roundhouse was shoddy and spent. Assorted stains blotted the frayed maroon carpet and the air was musty. With each step I encountered a different scent—first coffee, then sweat, then urine, then French fries. When the odor of vomit made me gag,

I looked down just in time to avoid stepping into a puddle of greenish-yellow slime. I held my breath and strode as quickly as I could to the arraignment room.

The chamber was packed. The defense attorneys, most of them wearing rumpled suits and shirts with frayed collars, looked anxiously at their watches and made small talk. The prosperous lawyers, in designer suits and Rolex watches, assembled in their own groups. The latter smiled broadly and exchanged banter with each other and the court personnel as if they had all the time in the world. They were being paid by the hour or receiving hefty fees to appear at the arraignment.

At the front of the room, a hassled public defender was hunched over the defense table sifting through a mountain of folders. Every few minutes he pushed back strands of blond hair that spilled over his forehead. He had to prepare for the dozens of defendants he would represent that morning—those unable to afford a "real" lawyer, as the defendants would often remind him.

The cadre of court personnel, both men and women, wore burgundy jackets and matching ties. Having little to do and owing their jobs to political patronage, they chatted about the weather or yawned. In the real world, they were either destined to fail or had failed already. That much was clear from their phlegmatic faces and listless gazes—and the self-importance with which they performed their menial tasks.

The families and friends of those who had been arrested filled the spectator seats. Some wore anxious expressions, while others were clearly irritated by being inconvenienced yet again by some wayward relation. A few dozen police officers, identifiable either by their uniforms or by their mismatched sport jackets and slacks, sat in the front rows.

My pulse raced as I walked towards the prosecutor's table. When I saw a young black ADA sitting there by himself, tapping his pen on a neat pile of files, my heart fell. But then I saw Carol seated in a chair behind him. She seemed lost in thought. At first glance, she looked exactly as she had the last time I saw her. Shoulder-length auburn hair gently brushed the top of her beige suit jacket. Her long legs were crossed and revealed just the proper amount of thigh. The silhouette of her cheekbones and the fullness of her lips were untouched by the passage of time. But when she tilted her head forward to speak to her fellow prosecutor, I saw a streak of gray hair. Time had not stood still. But, at nearly forty, she remained a beauty.

I was only a few feet away when she saw me. "David!" When she stood, her contoured suit displayed her familiar fit figure. She held out her hand and smiled. "How are you?" I took her hand in mine and held it longer than I should have.

"I'm fine. It's great to see you. You look terrific," I said. I stood back, pretending to appraise her for the first time.

"You don't look so bad yourself," she grinned.

Besides my thinning hair, I hadn't changed much. I hadn't gained much weight and I still had the fair skin that accompanies a freckled face, though most of my freckles were gone. "Thanks," I said.

A murmur behind me drew me back to thoughts of Feig. The court would soon be in session. "Carol, have you given any thought to our discussion yesterday?"

"Yes, I have, and—"

Before she could finish her sentence, the court crier bellowed, "Hear ye!"

I recognized the judge's name and, as he approached the bench, I looked into his middle-aged face and saw traces of the young man I had known.

The Honorable Bernard G. Rothenberg had recently won a term on the Court of Common Pleas in Philadelphia. Like most who ascend to the bench in the Commonwealth, he did so by playing politics. And, like all new judges, he had to pay his dues—which meant sitting in arraignment court disposing of cases at a superhuman pace.

Bernie and I went back to our high school days, when he was known as the school "bookie." Bernie used to cut his last class so he could make it to the afternoon horse races. He'd sneak into the track with a fake ID and lay the bets the rest of us put down at lunch. For his trouble, Bernie took a percentage of any winnings and a small handling fee from the losers.

After high school, where neither Bernie nor I distinguished ourselves, we both attended Temple University. But, at the sprawling campus in the heart of North Philadelphia, we went our separate ways. I cracked the books and, for the first time, achieved grades reflecting my abilities. Bernie, on the other hand, ran the football pools for the frats on Greek Row.

Although I hadn't seen Bernie in years, he was one of those wealthy lawyers everyone loves to hate so I'd heard plenty about him. His proclivity for taking risks paid off in his career—he seemed to prefer the potentially large contingency fee over a guaranteed hourly rate or contract fee. It was betting horses all over again. He hit it big with personal injury cases—first chasing ambulances and then pursuing doctors until he earned a reputation as the foremost medical malpractice attorney in the city. The rumor was that the medical community in Philadelphia so despised him that, when Bernie needed a hernia operation, he went to New York.

My guess was that Bernie had grown weary of negotiating settlements. Very few of his cases ever went to trial because, once the insurers saw him, they nearly always decided that a settlement was the prudent course of action. Even after a costly divorce and with a new "trophy" wife on his arm, Bernie seemed to have more money than he knew what to do with. Though he was always popular—and he was a likable sort—I think what he yearned for more than anything was respect. And what better way to command respect than to wield the power of the law?

Bernie bought thousand-dollar tickets to every political fundraiser, donated substantial sums of soft money to the party in power, and, according to the scuttlebutt, was not above stuffing wads of cash into politicians' pockets. He received his reward when the Democrats put him on the ticket. He won the election and became the Honorable Bernard G. Rothenberg.

As I watched him settle into his seat of power, I smiled. In high school he'd been the only one to don slacks and polo shirts, and in the courtroom he'd always tried to impress the jurors with custom-made suits and monogrammed shirts. But, no matter what he wore, he couldn't help being a slob. The Honorable Bernard G. Rothenberg was in desperate need of a haircut. His dark hair curled at the base of his neck and fell over his ears. His face sported a two-day stubble and his tie hung askew from an unbuttoned collar. Even from my vantage point behind the prosecutor's table I could see that the sleeve of his robe was besmirched with yellow blotches. It was probably mustard from a hot pastrami on rye—always one of Bernie's favorites. I envisioned him wolfing down the sandwich in chambers, engrossed in the sports page and planning his wagers on upcoming games.

As we took our seats, a door opened and the first group of defendants was led into the courtroom. Feig stood out among them as the only elderly white man, but there was something else. In contrast to the woeful countenances of the men and women surrounding him, Feig wore a defiant glare. He was a man, his glowering blue eyes said, who would not accept injustice. He scanned the courtroom until he found me.

I met his gaze and gave him a nod, as if to say, "Don't worry, I'll take it from here." Feig blinked, jettisoned his bravado, and I watched a great weariness pass over him. As his shoulders slumped, just a little, I saw his desire to give up. He wanted someone to take him by the hand and lead him to safety because he no longer had the strength to do it for himself. And that someone was me.

The crier called the first case and I turned away from Feig. Twenty minutes and four dispositions later, Commonwealth v. Jacob Feig was announced. Carol replaced the neophyte ADA at the prosecutor's desk and Feig and I took our positions at the defendant's table. I patted his sloped shoulder and leaned in to whisper that everything would be all right.

"Mr. Gold." Bernie gazed down at me, bristly eyebrows raised in amusement. "I see you have entered your appearance for the defendant."

"That's correct, Your Honor." The last two words stuck in my throat.

"It's been a while, eh, Mr. Gold?"

"Indeed, it has."

"Going to the reunion next year?"

I quickly calculated—could it have been a quarter of a century since we had graduated from high school? I had never attended a reunion and had no intention of ever doing so, but I didn't want to alienate him. No doubt, he was looking forward to flaunting his judgeship.

"I'm sure I will, and I look forward to seeing you there, Your Honor." Once again, I had to force the honorific out of my mouth.

"So, what have we here, uh, Ms. Silverberg?"

"Murder in the First Degree, Your Honor," Carol said.

But Bernie wasn't listening; his eyes were scanning the police report. He glanced at Feig and saw a disheveled old man with white whiskers being propped up with my hand at his elbow. Bernie had always been a quick study. He saw the world in black and white and made up his mind quickly. Nothing Carol or I had to say would make a difference. He finished perusing the slim folder and looked down at me.

"Your plea?"

"Not guilty," I said on Feig's behalf. "Your Honor," I began. I wanted to get my point across before Carol could speak. "The charge is ludicrous. If my client is culpable of anything, it's aiding a suicide. There are extenuating circumstances—"

"You can argue all that later, Mr. Gold. I just want to hear about bail."

"Mr. Feig is established in the community and not likely to run away. This has been his home for many years— he found his way here after he was liberated from Auschwitz." There was nothing in the folder to indicate that Feig was a Holocaust survivor, and I wanted Bernie to know. "I'm asking that the defendant be released on his own recognizance."

"That's absurd, Your Honor," Carol interjected. "This is a homicide, and bail is in order."

I was pleased she wasn't asking for a specific amount. That would give Bernie leeway.

"Approach." Bernie waved for us to stand before him, out of earshot of the gallery. "Listen, Davey." I flinched when Bernie called me by the name he used in high school. "There has to be bail. No two ways about it. I can't let your client walk on 'ROR.' Believe me, I don't want to see a man who survived Auschwitz get shanked awaiting trial in these sewers we call our prisons. But we have to be realistic. How much can he afford?"

"He can't afford anything, Your Honor."

"Doesn't he own a home?"

"No."

"Well, he's paying you, isn't he?"

"We haven't discussed that yet."

Bernie raised his eyebrows, but he knew me well enough to know I wasn't lying.

"Your Honor." Carol leaned forward. "What the defendant can or cannot afford is not the issue."

Bernie brushed her contention aside and returned to me. "Then what can you afford, Davey?"

"Me?"

"Yes you."

I pretended to be taken aback. I had already performed the calculations, adding the balances in my money market and checking accounts. I didn't want to sell the few stocks and bonds I owned, and I couldn't invade my retirement account without getting clobbered in taxes.

"Well, I could put up $20,000," I said.

Bernie's head bounced back. He was clearly incredulous that this was the extent of my liquidity. "Oh, all right." He shooed us back.

"Bail is set at twenty thousand dollars, cash or bond!" Bernie thundered and pounded his gavel. "Next matter." He flung Feig's file at his clerk, who caught it in midair.

"David," Feig croaked. "I don't have twenty—"

"Don't worry, Jacob. I do. Just don't run anywhere," I said, forcing a smile and patting Feig on the shoulder.

"Oh, David, this is too good of you. I can't allow you to do this but I don't want to go back to—"

The sheriff grabbed Feig by the arm and hauled him off to the holding tank.

"I'll have you out as soon as the paperwork is complete," I shouted to Feig.

I had hoped that Carol and I could have lunch, but she had a plea to take later in the morning and a jury panel to pick in the afternoon. "I'll take a rain check, Da-vee," she teased.

"No one's called me that in twenty years." I grimaced.

She grinned, taking delight in my chagrin.

"Thanks for not demanding a higher bail. I don't think I would have been able to swing it."

"It wouldn't have mattered what I said. Rothenberg's mind is made of stone. No way to change it once he makes a decision. But don't take this as a sign I'm rolling over and playing dead. You should seriously consider taking a plea and we can talk about minimal jail time."

"No time." I was surprised by my curt response, and so was Carol. "I can't let this man go to prison," I added. An awkward silence followed.

"Whatever you say, David. But you may want to reconsider." She took a few steps away. This is not how I wanted our first meeting in a decade to end. But then she turned. "Call me and we'll set a date for lunch," she said. "But only if we don't talk shop." She smiled, and she was off.

"Or maybe dinner?" I called after her. But I wasn't sure she heard.

It wasn't until late in the day that I finally retrieved Feig. I had to drive back to my office to transfer funds from my money market to my attorney account. Then I drove back to the Roundhouse with a check and waited in line for half an hour. After another ten minutes, the bulbous-nosed clerk finally unearthed Feig's paperwork. I signed the check and slid it under the glass.

"Can't take no personal checks. Gotta be a money order, bank check or certified unless you're a bail bondsman. You a bail bondsman?" The clerk smirked at me. His face was pock-marked.

"I'm an attorney—an officer of the court. The check is drawn on my attorney account."

The clerk stared at me and sighed. I could see a vague recollection pass over his face. Yes, he was allowed to accept lawyers' checks. And it was getting late and he had important things to do. Go to the bar for a few beers. Head home. Eat dinner. Watch television with the wife. Go to sleep. He took my check.

An hour later, Feig was in my car and we were on our way to his house. We spoke very little at first. We were both exhausted, though he had much more cause for fatigue.

"They piss just like pigs, David, right on the floor. It was terrible."

"Who did?"

"The *schvartzers*."

I flinched at his use of the pejorative epithet referring to blacks.

"They called me an old Jew when I complained, and they pushed and shoved me around from one to the other laughing, calling me 'Jew bastard' and 'kike.'"

"They didn't hurt you, did they?" I glanced at him, but other than a visible weariness he appeared unharmed.

"You know, at Auschwitz the anti-Semites were on the other side of the fence. You didn't have to worry about having your throat slit while you slept. At least we had that." Out of the corner of my eye, I saw Feig's cynical smile. Then his mouth clamped shut and his lips tightened. "I can't go back. No more bars or wire fences."

"Don't worry," I said. "You won't have to." I tried to sound confident.

"Why should I not worry? Because you are a lawyer and you believe in justice?" I could hear the sneer in his words. "There is no justice in the world, you know. How could there be? And if there ever was justice, David, it died— along with God—at Auschwitz. I assure you of that."

"It's different now. At least it is here," I said. I knew full well that a statue of a jowl-faced, cigar-chomping fat man on his knees rolling the dice would more accurately reflect our legal system than the blindfolded woman gripping the sword of justice. And yet I did believe that at least a smidgen of justice remained—though often one had to labor mightily to unearth it.

"No, David, it's no different in America. Only a matter of time and circumstance. Another Great Depression, a modern-day plague, or perhaps a rising tide of religious

fervor, will remind the good citizens of the Christ-killers
in their midst. The only place where Jews are safe is among
their own—in *Eretz Yisrael*. I would never have left if I hadn't
met Ilse."

There was no dissuading him, and I felt I had no right
to try to change his mind. He had come to his convictions
through terrible suffering. But I did feel that I needed to
know more of his story.

"What about Auschwitz? You still haven't told me
what happened there." In the silence that greeted my question I glanced over at him. His square jaw had snapped shut.
I detected a slight tremor in his chin and lips, but they never
parted.

"I'm tired," he finally said. "But we will speak of this
soon, I promise. You are entitled to that, my friend, if you
want to hear of it."

I spent the rest of the journey trying to reassure Feig
that everything would work out, but I could offer nothing
concrete to bolster my claim.

"Let's plan to meet in a few days," I said as we pulled
up in front of his house.

"I don't know how to thank you," he said. His voice
wavered. He stepped out of the car and stood for a moment
gazing at the dark, empty house, as if deciding whether or
not to go inside. But where else could he go? Nor was that
the first time that Feig, having had no home to return to after
the War, faced such a dilemma. There was only one thing a
man like him could do—take one step at a time. He walked
down the path leading to his front door.

I waited while he fumbled for his keys and let himself in before I drove away. All the way home I tried to think
about Feig and how to spare him a prison sentence. But my

thoughts kept returning to Carol, to her smile and her sparkling green eyes. She seemed to have changed so little, and I realized that the feelings I had buried so long ago had not changed either.

As soon as I entered my dark apartment, I saw the red light flashing on my answering machine. There were three messages. One from a telemarketer and two from my mother. "Call me back as soon as you get in, David," her second message said. "No matter what time it is."

I fumbled with the familiar number. What could be wrong?

"Is everything all right?" I asked as soon as she answered the phone.

"Yes, David. Why shouldn't it be?"

"You're OK? Dad's OK?"

"Everything's fine. Why are you so upset?"

"Because you left two messages and asked me to call you back no matter how late—that's why!"

"I only wanted to talk with you."

"About what?"

"How are you?"

"I'm fine. Is that why you called?"

"Do I need a reason to talk to my son?"

"Of course not." I took a deep breath. "I'm fine, Mom, just a little tired. Had a tough day. You and Dad OK?"

"I said we are."

"How's the weather?"

"It rained a bit today, but your father and I still got our swimming in and we just came back from dinner."

"Good. Now, may I ask why you called?"

"David, you won't believe what I came upon."

"What?"

"Oma's diary—the one she kept in Theresienstadt."

"Oma kept a diary?" I was shocked. "And we never knew?" I pictured her room, the bookshelf, the photographs. Where had she kept this diary?

"Oh, I knew she'd written a diary. I've had it ever since she died."

"I thought you said you just came upon it."

"I did. I'd packed it away when we moved to Florida. You know how I never like to throw things out. I got around to opening the box last week."

"But you've been living in Florida for years!" I said. "Mom, I can't believe you never told me about this."

I could almost see her shrug. "That's why I'm calling you, David. I'm going to mail it to you tomorrow."

"Oh no, don't do that. Let's wait until my next visit. I don't want it to get lost in the mail."

"But I want you to have it now. I've included some notes translating it as best as I could."

"Then at least insure it and keep the tracking number."

"OK."

"I still can't believe you kept this from me all these years."

"When you read it, David, you'll see why." Her tone had changed. She was wary, hesitant—as if she wasn't sure she was doing the right thing.

"What do you mean?"

"You'll see. I just feel you should have it. And David? I don't ever want to talk about this again."

"All right," I said, "but I don't understand."

A few days later, after immersing myself in the lives of my grandparents and their time at Terezin, I understood.

8

The brown paper wrapping fell to the floor as I seized the small black journal, which was about the size of my hand and no more than half an inch thick. Its binding was bent and broken, its black cloth cover stained and frayed. As I examined it, half a dozen pages fell to the floor. My mother's handwriting covered each one—tiny letters squeezed into tight lines on both sides, no margins. This was her translation.

For several minutes I stood gripping my grandmother's journal in trembling hands. The knowledge that I was holding a piece of Oma and Opa's nightmare in Theresienstadt, half a century later, overwhelmed me. My grandmother never spoke of that terrible time and now, after she was dead, I was about to hear her story—as though she'd be speaking to me from the grave. I put the book down, shuddered, and walked away.

Dreams plagued my sleep that night. The next day the diary remained where I had set it, though it never left my mind. When I returned from work I opened the diary, spread my mother's notes on the table along with a German-English dictionary I had purchased, and began to read. The diary began in Oma's steady hand that gradually, over the course of their time in Theresienstadt, deteriorated to an almost unintelligible scrawl.

Between the German I still remembered speaking as a boy, my study of the language in high school, my mother's effort at translation, and the dictionary, the story of my grandparents' two and a half years in Theresienstadt unfolded. Like a bear drawn to a beehive's honey, I could not pull myself away from the story. And only when I had reached its end the next morning, with the sun's first rays on the horizon, did I slide the diary to a far corner of the table, drop my head, and fall into a deep slumber.

Though the words were Oma's and the translation my mother's, the voice that I heard was my own—as though I were telling myself the story. This story would sear my soul with an indelible mark not dissimilar from the bluish-green numbers branded on Feig's forearm. I've told the tale to myself many times since and will, no doubt, recount it many more times—perhaps even to others. But it always begins the same way.

Sometime late in the afternoon of October 9, 1942, a train pulled into a station outside the Czechoslovakian town of Terezin, a village consisting of two hundred and nineteen dilapidated and neglected homes. An eerie quiet greeted the rolling rail cars as they screeched to a halt on the rusted tracks. Suddenly, shouts of "*Schnell! Macht Schnell!*" shattered the stillness. German soldiers in drab gray coats strutted through the small depot like warlords. Czech police in green uniforms groveled alongside the Germans, echoing the cry for those debarking to make haste.

The disembarking passengers hardly noticed a handful of Jewish police huddled in a remote corner. Because they wore red conductor caps, they were easily mistaken for railway employees. Nor did the Jews who were just arriving pay much attention to the four SS men dressed in black leather jackets and smoking cigarettes. With twisted grins planted on their frozen faces, the SS men coolly observed the people bumbling and tripping over each other as though they were clowns in a circus.

Among the several hundred German Jews detraining as the sun set behind a distant line of trees were my grandparents, Sophie and Ludwig. As were their fellow travelers, they were taken aback at the brusqueness with which they were treated. After all, Sophie thought, according to the authorities who notified them to pack their belongings and prepare to leave immediately, this transfer was to be nothing more than a "change of address."

"Where are we going?" Sophie had asked. She had squared her shoulders and stepped between the smug German officer and her husband, who had fallen back into the shadows of their one-room residence in the Jewish quarter.

"To a lovely place called Theresenbad or, as some say, Theresienstadt am See," the young man said, describing a lovely village on the lake. "It is like Carlsbad, Frau. Indeed, it is not far from Carlsbad. A health spa, Frau!" But she detected a sinister glimmer in his black eyes and the upturn of his thin lips was more a sneer than a smile. "Pack your suitcases with care," the blond soldier shouted over his shoulder as he departed.

Sophie had lived her entire life in Germany, so she was anxious to learn all she could about where she and her husband were headed. After making a number of inquiries, she learned that Theresienstadt, located north of Prague and not far from the German border, had been recently designated a Jewish town. There German-speaking Jews over sixty could live the remainder of their lives. In addition, Jews who had served the *Vaterland* in World War I and were disabled or decorated also qualified for residency. So being sent to Theresienstadt seemed logical, Sophie concluded, since Ludwig was sixty, a decorated war veteran, and still easily agitated due to the poison gas he had inhaled in the trenches. Moreover, the move seemed auspicious given the terrible rumors she had heard about the destinations in the East where most of her friends and family had been deported.

At the train station, Sophie became apprehensive when the soldiers instructed the passengers to line up for a medical inspection. She tugged at the short sleeve of her dress to try and cover her swollen arm where she injected herself daily with insulin for diabetes. She worried that the disease might prevent her from being admitted into the town, but her fears were allayed when she saw the friendly face of the Jewish physician conducting the cursory examinations. She assumed that the doctor's red and white armband signaled that he was Jewish. "K. L. Terezin" was written in the center of the band, and the name "Dr. Reines" ran down the side in cursive letters. Sophie and Ludwig would soon receive similar armbands inscribed with their names.

"Will I be able to secure insulin here?" she asked after Dr. Reines noticed the bulge on her arm.

"I'm afraid not, Frau. But do not be concerned. The diet in Terezin works wonders on diabetics! None of the sweets and harmful foods to raise your sugar are available." The physician forced a laugh but, when he saw her bewildered face, he returned to his task. He knew that she would soon learn all about the diet in Terezin. Dr. Reines appraised Ludwig with a glance and returned to Sophie "You both can move on. No need for a ride on the truck. You two can walk with the rest."

He dismissed them both with a wave of his hand. So this was not a selection process, like the ones she had heard whispered about, where the unfit were deported East. Sophie sighed with relief. The examination was only to see if she and

Ludwig could walk to the town. She thought how kind it was that they provided transportation for those unable to walk.

With typical German efficiency, the bulk of the newcomers were ordered into rows four abreast and, clutching their baggage, they commenced the trek to their new home situated somewhere on the horizon. The procession bypassed the houses of the Czechoslovakian population and tramped directly to the fortress Theresienstadt.

During the march, Sophie learned from the murmurs of those around her what rumors suggested about their new quarters. The Jewish ghetto was located inside a fortress built by the Austrian Emperor Joseph II and named in honor of his mother, Empress Maria Theresa. From the end of the eighteenth century onward, the fortress had been used as military barracks, with quarters for officers and their families. It functioned like a small town with stores, a post office, a church, and even a hotel.

When Sophie first glimpsed the imposing granite walls covered with grass and the trees looming in the distance, she could not have known that the fortress was in the shape of an eight-pointed star. Only later did she learn the simple layout of the garrison town with its five vertical streets and twelve cross streets.

As the weary procession skirted the swampland, Sophie shivered in the cold damp air. The deep moats surrounding the fortress exacerbated the dank smell and soggy atmosphere. The marchers grumbled as they plodded, still four abreast, under the archway leading into the fortress.

Sophie wondered if there would be an official delegation to greet them. Would thousands of Jewish men, women, and children be going about their business as they would in any city? Or would people be in their homes, having supper and perhaps preparing for bed? After all, she realized, it was late.

But Sophie was not prepared for what awaited her and the hundreds of other Jews passing through the fortress's walls for the first time. Dr. Siegfried Seidel, the ghetto's first commandant, imposed a strict curfew on every arrival day. Despite his slips into sadism, the Jewish population would miss Seidel after the notorious and brutal Anton Burger replaced him the following year.

As night fell, Sophie and Ludwig gazed in a daze at the dark and barren streets. They felt as though they had entered a ghost town. The only sounds they heard were the shuffling of feet and the occasional scrape of luggage along the cobblestones. Sophie's feet felt so heavy she was relieved when the procession came to a halt. They stood outside the door of a bleak stone building that served as the absorption center. They entered one by one as officials matched their names to a list and crossed them off.

There were strict procedures to follow. Luggage was checked. All money and jewelry was confiscated, including the gold watch my grandfather had received on his bar mitzvah. Here, somehow, he concealed the silver pocket watch I eventually inherited. Dr. Reines supervised physical examinations and, once again, assured my grandmother that she would fare well without her insulin injection.

Finally, at the end of the third day, the intake operation was complete. Transports had begun arriving in June, and by New Year's day, 1943, over 109,000 "favored" Jews had marched into the fortress—and over half of them had died from disease, beatings, execution, or from being transported East.

Officials at the absorption center gave everyone ration slips and assigned jobs and living quarters. The men were housed in the Sudenten barracks—an immense three-story building at the periphery of the ghetto. The women and children were directed to the Hamburger and Dresden barracks—three-story buildings covering an entire block. Cries of protest and tears of anguish filled the absorption center as families were torn asunder.

When Sophie saw the terror in her husband's eyes she insisted on speaking to someone in authority. She explained how the roar of cannons had impaired her husband's hearing while he was serving his country. "And he was decorated! Is this how he is to be repaid?" she asked. The placid expression that the staff representative from the Council of Elders wore remained unchanged.

But the German officer peering over the Jewish official's shoulder took interest. "You say your husband was decorated, Frau?"

She looked up at the German officer, a man in his fifties with a gray mustache who, she thought, must have seen duty in the First World War. "Yes," she answered.

As the German turned to Ludwig, Sophie detected a glint of recognition in his gaze. Had the Jew standing before him been one of his comrades in the trenches? Perhaps this old Jew was the young officer who had pulled him out of harm's way when he was lying wounded atop a heap of bodies. The German whispered into the Jewish official's ear. The Jew shrugged and wrote new instructions on a slip of paper.

After wandering the ghetto's dark streets for more than an hour, Sophie and Ludwig located their living quarters in a building crammed with families of the staff serving the Council of Elders. They climbed three flights of narrow creaking stairs to a large open area. It was difficult to judge the size of the room because of the sheets, hanging from the ceiling that separated one family from another.

People scurried everywhere, but no one acknowledged their presence. A cacophony of languages caused Sophie's head to swirl. Most were speaking High German but, as they made their way through the throng, she could tell that many of the Jews were from Czechoslovakia and Hungary. Later, the dormitory would also be home to Jews from the Netherlands, Luxembourg, and Denmark.

Just as she was about to give up hope of finding a place to sleep, she spotted an unoccupied space in a far corner that was perhaps two meters wide by two meters long. A ragged mattress balanced precariously on a makeshift box spring pushed up against the moldy wall. There was barely enough room for them to stand after they dropped their luggage on the floor. But they would make do, she resolved. She could not have imagined, that first sleepless night, that this corner would be their home for the next two and a half years, or that they would become used to the foul-smelling, clammy air and the stench of unwashed bodies. Neither could she have imagined even more people living in this room—so many more that they would be assigned shifts for sitting or lying down on the sodden floors.

Except for the visits of the Red Cross, there was little variation in the daily routine. Every morning, Sophie and Ludwig queued up to receive a breakfast of ersatz coffee and their daily allotment of a half-loaf of black bread. In the afternoon, they were served soup—either a tasteless lentil soup or a weak soup called *wrucken* with white turnips and a mixture of sand, dirt, and a trace of flour to give it substance. Sipping her ersatz coffee, Sophie took some comfort that the absence of sugar would indeed keep her diabetes in check.

While Sophie and Ludwig eventually grew accustomed to the cold damp air and the incessant gnawing of an empty stomach, the loss of privacy was something else. There were people everywhere. Long lines of people with sunken faces and haunted eyes filled the courtyards—waiting to be fed, or to receive rations, or to petition the Council with some special request. In the midst of this suffering and despair, Sophie was amazed and delighted to hear the shouts of children at play and to watch them run about. As she prayed that they'd remain oblivious to their fate, she prayed for her daughter—my mother. And she remembered how she had loved to romp in the backyard of their home. She tried not to worry about her daughter, so far away, or to dwell on their home, now lost and probably in the hands of a Gentile family who had admired it from afar and who had jumped at the opportunity to snatch it up at the bargain price set by the Nazis.

Sometimes, late in the afternoon or in the early evening, a singer or musician filled the air with music. Once the ghetto organized itself, there were periodic entertainment and cultural activities. A Theresienstadt symphony performed on a regular basis, several artist studios were opened, and a makeshift library was set up.

But of all the activities that this isolated Jewish community established, the vibrant religious life was most precious to Sophie. Two months after she and Ludwig passed through the ramparts of Theresienstadt, Dr. Leo Baeck, the former chief rabbi of Berlin and the unofficial spiritual leader of Germany's Jews, arrived. With his high forehead and white beard, even when shouldering a pushcart, Baeck cut an imposing figure and soon became the ghetto's rabbi. Sophie would exclaim to Ludwig what an honor it was each time they joined the venerable rabbi in prayers. In spite of everything, her faith in God never diminished.

In time, the Jewish ghetto of Terezin evolved into a little city just as the Germans had envisioned. Still, however, there was no escape from the ceaseless conversations, screaming, yelling, and crying that permeated every nook and cranny of the town. Sophie's greatest desire, second only to seeing her daughter, was for some peace and quiet.

She was assigned to tend the gardens that the Council of Elders hoped would provide fresh vegetables for the populace. Ludwig, whose experience as a cattle broker was of little value to his new community, was assigned to maintenance details. While he was not happy performing menial work, he accepted his new lot. He lived day by day and had little interest in the goings-on of the ghetto that didn't directly affect his immediate needs.

Sophie, on the other hand, wanted to learn how the Jewish hierarchy in Theresienstadt was constituted. Who made the important decisions? How much power—if any—did the Jews in authority wield? Or were they merely puppets for the SS? This was not idle curiosity, for she feared that the time would come when her life, and that of her husband, might depend upon knowing this power structure. Eventually, she was able to glean the information she sought.

The Jewish leadership was known as the Council of Elders. At first, Jews from Prague made up this body but, as transports arrived from Germany, German Jews also took seats on the Council. The first man to lead the Council was Jakob Edelstein, who arrived from Prague in December 1941 and was involved in developing the Jewish municipality from the ground up. With his thick dark wavy hair and egg-shaped glasses, Edelstein was easy to spot as he strode through the ghetto's streets dutifully listening to petitioners along the way. The German authorities sometimes mockingly referred to him as the "Elder of the Jews," but he did have influence on the ghetto's operation. Edelstein's name was well known to everyone if for no other reason than that the paper money marked with the Star of David that became the ghetto's currency bore his signature.

The office of the Council of Elders and its staff was located in the Magdeburger barracks. Also situated in these quarters were one- and two-room apartments where each member of the Council lived with his family. During the day, when their wives and children attended to work, chores, and school classes, a Council member could steal away into the quiet and privacy of his apartment. They also sometimes used these apartments for other, clandestine, purposes.

There were two things, Sophie soon learned, to avoid at all costs. First, being singled out for some infraction or detained for punishment was usually a death sentence. Those hapless souls were incarcerated in a brown brick building that once served as a prison but that, in Terezin, functioned as a concentration camp. The "Little Fortress," as it was called, was located only a short distance from town and was operated by the Gestapo, the SS, and kapos, or prisoner functionaries. No Jew ever escaped the Little Fortress, and only a few prisoners were released. Most who entered were never seen again.

The other thing Sophie learned to avoid was selection for a transport heading East. The *Ostentransporte*, or East Transports as they were referred to in furtive whispers among Terezin's population, were organized according to a strict procedure. Four days before departure, the Council of Elders summoned those selected and informed them that they would be boarding trains bound for the East, where they would work at labor camps. At first, there was no reason to doubt this explanation. But when no word was ever heard from those boarding the *Ostentransporte* and rumors of all sorts abounded, the people came to understand that mounting the steps of a transport was also a death sentence.

Until the summer of 1944 when the Germans took on the task for themselves, the Council of Elders determined which names to place on the lists for transport. Through the night, and often well into the morning hours, the Council would agonize and argue, struggling to agree on a list of names. They made every effort to spare the young.

"They're our future!" someone would invariably shout during a stormy session.

"But the young are strong and more likely to survive a labor camp," someone else might retort. "And what is here for them, anyway? Disease and a slow death? Maybe in a labor camp there's more food. How else can the Nazis expect one to work?"

Guffaws and rolling eyes generally greeted such logic. "Labor camps! A joke! A trick! They work you to death! Everyone knows they're death camps."

"The War will end. It's only a matter of time for an Allied victory. The youth will live for us."
Or so they hoped.

The elders on the Council were expected to be objective, and yet they were only human. How could they not spare their family and friends? And what of the friends of family and the friends of friends?

Everyone tried to ingratiate himself with one or more members of the Council or someone on their staff.

Corruption was unavoidable. It might take the form of a promise to share a stash of jewelry left behind with a trusted Gentile friend, or an offer of partnership in a thriving business that could easily be re-established after the War, or cash to be withdrawn from a secret bank account. Sometimes it was nothing more than sliding a pack of cigarettes or Terezin currency across the table. Sometimes there were other, more personal, favors.

At first, Sophie and Ludwig did not concern themselves with the transports since everyone over the age of sixty was excluded. Though only Ludwig met this requirement, they knew that efforts were customarily made to keep married couples together. Nor were they alarmed when the age was raised to sixty-five, since they were preferred Germans because of Ludwig's war record.

At times, Sophie imagined they would never be summoned because no one knew they were residents of Terezin. Hadn't they become practically invisible? They resided in the Council's staff quarters but were not staff; they disappeared every day to perform tasks that drew no one's attention; they didn't have a large family; and they were growing so gaunt with each passing month that Sophie fantasized they just might vanish into thin air and, like clouds, float to freedom.

So it came as a shock in early 1944 when Sophie learned that Ludwig had been placed on the list for transport. What astounded her even more was the reason he'd been selected.

"Water? My husband is to go on the *Ostentransporte* because of water?" She struggled to maintain dignity and calm as she steadied herself before the elder seated behind his desk. She didn't want him to see how furious she was—or how frightened. "What do you mean by 'water'?" she asked.

The man with the oval face leaned back in his chair and tugged at his mustache. His flabby neck rolled over his stiff white collar and tightly knotted tie. Ludwig had always worn ties, even at home, but not here—not anymore. And though Ludwig had once carried a few extra pounds, he carried them well. Sophie watched this man, wearing his weight like blubber on a seal, and seethed.

"Are you not ashamed that you remain fat while others starve?" she wanted to shout. "Be a leader! Refuse extra rations! Or give them to the children!" But she held her tongue and waited.

"Your husband, Frau, has repeatedly violated our rules concerning the rationing of water. Other than once a month, showers are strictly prohibited except for exceptional circumstances. Yet—"The little man stopped for a moment and wiped the sweat from his brow with a fleshy hand. "Yet your husband showered at least four times last month, and that is only what we know of. And this has been a pattern, Frau. It has been going on for quite some time. We cannot tolerate it any longer."The man looked up from his papers and glared.

"I am sorry, but my husband requires regular showers," Sophie explained calmly. "After the War, the months in the trenches, the nerve gas, he's phobic about dirt."

"Do I look like Freud to you, Frau?"The man chuckled. "I couldn't care less about your husband's need to shower. He must make do with hand washing. We all do."

"Not you! Not your wife and children!" she wanted to scream as she throttled the man by his flabby jowls. But, once more, she restrained herself. She saw that trying to convince this man to remove her husband's name from the list by appealing to his compassion would be fruitless. It was time to charm him. She was good at getting people to do what she wanted them to do.

In the ghetto as they had been at her home, people were drawn to Sophie. She was kind-hearted, and her voice was soft and alluring. Even in her mid-fifties she was still a striking woman. Beyond a few wrinkles and strands of gray, the dark-haired beauty—a Jewish Aphrodite—was still visible. Her brown eyes glistened; her high cheekbones remained regal; her satiny neck was still inviting.

"Herr, please. What can I do to keep my husband with me? I'll make certain that he will not shower more than—"

"I'm sorry, Frau. The list is complete. There is nothing I can do." The rotund man squirmed.

"Then add my name," Sophie said. She squared her shoulders. "I will accompany my husband. It is your policy to keep husband and wife together, is it not?"

"Not always, Frau. And please, do not sacrifice yourself."

"Add my name. If you do not, I will board the transport no matter what you say." The small man stared at her with his beady eyes. He must have known that she meant what she said. He couldn't bear to see this lovely lady in a forced labor camp being worked and starved to death—or worse. She was radiant and stately, even here in this ghetto. And yet there was a tenderness about her, a softness.

"Are you absolutely certain there's nothing I can do to have my husband's name removed from the list?" she asked again, leaning over the desktop.

He stroked his salt-and-pepper mustache and a leer spread over his mottled face. She looked him straight in the eyes. Without even glancing down at the paper, he struck Ludwig's name from the list. Ludwig was spared.

In her diary, she referred to this man only as Herr M.
The letter "M" could have been an initial or nothing at all. She
did not provide details of the assignations that followed, the
humiliation she endured, or how many times she had to give
herself to this vile man who wielded life and death over his
fellow Jews.

Perhaps what brought her through the horror of the
creaking bedsprings and the grunts of the clammy man bearing down upon her was a semblance of quiet. For these brief
times only, over her years at Terezin, there was no chattering,
no screaming, no cacophony of conversations in tongues she
did not always understand, no barking of orders. If she separated her mind from her body it was quiet enough to imagine
herself elsewhere—beyond the fortress walls and over the
ocean in America where, she prayed, her daughter was thriving.

Immediately prior to the Red Cross inspection in
June 1944, Herr M. disappeared from Theresienstadt—and
from the pages of Sophie's diary. Perhaps he succumbed to
disease, as hundreds did every week. If he displeased the
Germans in some way, he would have been dispatched to the
Little Fortress. Perhaps a member of the Council of Elders
with moral fiber found him out and put him on the list for
the next transport.

Herr M. vanished just about the time that orders
were given to transform Theresienstadt into the model ghetto
Hitler had promised—to prove to the world that he was
taking care of his Jews. Terezin's populace was put to work
constructing an elaborate facade designed to mask the reality
lurking behind it. It was not difficult to see through this facade, but the Red Cross delegation was not so inclined. Easily

deceived inspectors were impressed with the fresh flowers planted everywhere and the green shrubs hastily burrowed in soft brown dirt. They saw women with bronze skin tanned by the sun, Sophie among them, who laughed and sang with hoes over their shoulders as they strolled to the fields. They saw children at play. Any youngsters stopped by members of the delegation recited a carefully rehearsed script confirming how happy they were.

Days after the Red Cross completed their inspection, a German film crew moved into the ghetto. Why waste the carefully fabricated masquerade? Terezin was proof that the rumors of labor camps and killing camps had no foundation. They were a lie invented by American Jews. A propaganda movie, depicting the Jewish town just as the Red Cross delegation had observed it, was filmed so that the world could witness how happy Terezin's Jews really were.

Hours after the final reel of film was stowed away, the Council of Elders received orders to dismantle the illusion. Inmates were assigned to tear down the flimsy walls, rip up the shrubs, pull out the flowers, take apart the children's playground, and disassemble the stage in the center of the ghetto where musicians had performed. The inhabitants of the ghetto let out a collective sigh and braced themselves to accept the fact life would return to normal. But the Council of Elders knew better—things would never return to normal. Terezin was no longer needed for propaganda purposes. The Red Cross visit was a thing of the past. Theresienstadt became dispensable—as did its Jews.

9

As the summer of 1944 drew to a close, the Germans were furious when they learned that Jewish partisans had been joining the Czechoslovakian resistance. There were thirty thousand Jews living in Terezin and Karl Rahm, the new commandant, grew increasingly alarmed as the rumors circulated of an active underground preparing an uprising in the ghetto. After deliberations, the Germans decided to obliterate Theresienstadt by aerial bombardment and blame the Allies, whose planes were constantly overhead.

But the "Thousand-Year Reich" was caving in on itself. The Russians were closing in from the east, and the Americans and British were breaking through the fronts from the south and west. The German military had more important things on its mind than the murder of more Jews. And while killing Jews was still the number-one priority for the SS, it did not have access to aircraft bombers. Consequently, the inmates of Terezin were sentenced to be liquidated in the usual manner—transport to Auschwitz or death from disease and starvation.

In January 1945, however, something most extraordinary began to take shape. At first, no one paid much attention to rumors that the end of the War was at hand. But when days turned into weeks and no new transports left Terezin for the East, the speculation inside the ghetto grew. The Nazis were retreating in haphazard fashion all over Europe, people said. Hitler had been shot by partisans, another source proclaimed. No, another report said, the *Führer* was assassinated in a bunker by Goebbels himself, who had made a deal with the Allies to spare his family. Others heard that Berlin was already a smoldering pile of rubble and the Russians were racing the Americans to lay first claim to the victor's spoils.

But although no one inside Terezin knew exactly why the Council issued an official statement in February saying that it appeared safe to conclude there would be no transports East, the news brought a collective sigh of relief. Evidently there no longer was an "East" under German control, and speculation had it that there was no longer an "Auschwitz" either. The inmates heard and saw proof of this fact themselves when, in late March, a scraggly band of no more than thirty Jews shuffled through the archway of the fortress Theresienstadt. Sophie couldn't believe her eyes as she watched these walking skeletons.

A lone Nazi soldier, a youth not old enough to grow a full beard and carrying his rifle as a farmer would carry a hoe, led the group to Commandant Rahm's quarters. There a weary officer refused him entry. Sophie sidled along the wall, making herself invisible but getting close enough to hear the Germans arguing about who would assume responsibility for this handful of Jews who refused to die during the merciless march from Auschwitz.

Ultimately, the young soldier prevailed because there was no feasible alternative. Where else could these Jews be left? He would not shoot them, he declared. He was a soldier in the German army and did not kill unarmed civilians—even if they were *schutzige Juden*. Unlike the SS guards and kapos in his detachment, he proclaimed, he had never shot at the bodies falling by the wayside each day of the trek. And no, he would not continue to shepherd them because he was determined to rejoin his division, wherever that might be, to fight on for the *Vaterland und Der Führer*. As he said this he squared his shoulders and brought himself to full height—just below the chin of the man blocking his entry.

The impassive officer outside Rahm's quarters rolled his eyes and snickered at the young man's exuberance. Finally, with a chuckle, he offered the soldier a meal and a good night's sleep before departing in the morning to carry on the War. The lad followed him inside without so much as a backward glance at the shivering Jews huddled in the late winter's cold in this forsaken place.

Two years earlier, when Sophie and Ludwig had entered the fortress Theresienstadt, lists were meticulously checked and re-checked. But there was no list for this group. No groans or twisted, sneering Aryan mouths barking out Jewish names. As far as the Germans were concerned, this band of stragglers didn't exist. And yet somehow, despite multiple death sentences—beatings, shooting, gas, exhaustion, starvation, disease—they had survived.

The shivering stick-like figures rocked back and forth in unison but their feet were planted where they stood, as though an invisible fence confined them. Sophie took a few steps towards them but couldn't tell one from the other— not their ages or, in many cases, their gender. Their sunken eyes stared nowhere and their cheekbones protruded like glaciers on either side of their prominent noses. Their shaved heads sprouted haphazard strands of new growth. Rags hung on their bony frames and their shoulders quaked from the cold. Sophie looked down to see bloodied toes jutting from frayed makeshift footwear.

Sophie felt drawn to the face of a boy who was looking at her, or so she thought. She was walking over to him when two men from the Council, Danes who had arrived in late 1944, came upon the scene. From the cacophony of languages she pieced together that these Auschwitz survivors were from many different countries—Hungary, Denmark, Norway, Sweden, and even Germany. Their story was nothing short of incredible.

The Nazis had indeed fled Auschwitz, taking all the Jews with them except those too sick to stand who would die in a matter of hours or days anyway. The idea behind the journey, hundreds of miles in the brutal winter, was that most of the Jews would perish along the way. And those who did survive would be rewarded with extermination.

But this group had escaped both fates. In the confusion of a snow squall they splintered off from the main march and, under the direction of the young German soldier, they came instead to Theresienstadt.

The Danes from the Council decided not to wait for the Germans to determine what to do with these Jews. The Germans, after all, had abandoned them in the cold, unfed and left perhaps to die. The Danes led this collection of barely breathing cadavers to receive food and be assigned quarters.

But the boy Sophie had noticed did not follow the others. It was as if he was oblivious to what was happening. Perhaps he could not hear or understand what was said, or maybe he no longer cared. He continued to stare at her. The look in his eyes would haunt her until the day she died.

His narrow black eyes simmered like coal, fueled by a seething hatred that caused her to shudder. She supposed he was probably thirteen or fourteen. The adult bodies of his companions had shriveled to the point that they could just as easily have been children. And the faces of the young were so drawn and wizened that they could have been old men and women. A cruel trick had turned time upside down for these Jews. She walked over to fetch the boy.

As she did, a memory from another place and time came back to her. She remembered finding a baby sparrow that had fallen from its nest in her garden. Its mother was nowhere in sight, so she scooped the tiny fledgling into her hand. It's wriggling legs and tiny claws tickled and made her laugh. The bird's open beak frantically searched the air for something to eat. After settling the bird into a small box that she covered with grass in a sheltered spot on the porch, she fed it with moist bread crumbs and water through an eye dropper. After some days, the sparrow took its first tenuous steps. Later, it began hopping the length and width of the porch until finally, one day, it flapped its wings with sufficient force to lift its body into the air and fly off—without ever looking back.

Like the bird, the boy never spoke as Sophie and Ludwig tended to him in their corner compartment. Yet, somehow, they communicated. It wasn't a matter of a language barrier, since the boy seemed to have deserted the world of words altogether. He complied with Sophie's instructions. She showed him when and what to eat, when to sleep, when to shower and wash up, and when to clean the clothes he had been given—pants, shirt, and shoes left behind by boys his age who had been sent on transport or died from disease.

Despite the scarcity of decent provisions in the ghetto, the boy had been given so little nourishment for so long that, in time, he actually put on some weight and began to show some flesh on his bones. The other change was more subtle, and Sophie detected it only gradually. It was in his eyes.

The jet-black gloss of hatred slowly faded to a bold, bright azure glow. But the darkness did not disappear; it remained below the surface. Sophie imagined it lurking like a shark, swimming ceaselessly through the waters—never stopping to rest or sleep because it was not in its nature to do so. She shuddered when she allowed herself to ponder what horrors these eyes had witnessed, what secrets remained, what hatred lay buried.

She never saw him smile, laugh, cry, or scream in his sleep. He never displayed any emotion—nor did he focus on anything or anyone except Sophie, who hovered over him like a mother hen. He would stare at her saying nothing, and yet everything, with his eyes. She never heard him speak a single word. Not even on the day they parted.

My grandmother wrote her penultimate diary entry on May 9, 1945, the day Theresienstadt was liberated. She reported the event in the same matter-of-fact tone she used throughout the diary. The gates are open, she wrote. The Jews are free to go.

But there was nowhere to go, so they remained in Terezin. A month later, arrangements were finally made for relocation. After weeks of being sent from here to there, Sophie and Ludwig found themselves interned once again—this time in a Displaced Persons Center in Deggendorf.

The boy had been consigned to a different destination as soon as they left Terezin. Sophie and Ludwig had identities; they had each other; they had a former home (though it was unlikely that they could, or would, return to it); they had a daughter living in America who would receive them once arrangements could be made.

But the boy had no one and no identity, so he was sent elsewhere. Sophie, who recorded their parting in her last diary entry, remained undemonstrative—just as she had on the day she said goodbye to her daughter about to board the ship to America. No tears. Just a stiff hug and a smile and, perhaps, a prayer that, like the fledgling sparrow, the boy would find his wings and live a better life one day.

• • •

My grandmother didn't know the exact number, but her estimate of the number of Jews found alive in Terezin was uncannily close to the official tally of 16,832. Of these survivors, one-quarter died from dysentery and disease in the first few weeks following liberation. Of the 141,184 Jews who entered the "paradise" ghetto, only 12,000 survived. It was a minor miracle, if one is inclined to believe in miracles, that both my grandparents emerged as survivors to one day come to America and live with my parents and me. Yet they did.

10

When I awoke at the table the next morning, stiff and sore, the sun was high in the sky and the closed diary sat on the corner of the table where I'd left it. Physically exhausted and emotionally spent, I crawled into bed. But I couldn't fall back to sleep. Every time I closed my eyes, another image of Theresienstadt flashed before me. I shivered under the covers, feeling the chill of Terezin's dank air. I smelled mold growing on the walls. My empty stomach rumbled, yet I had no appetite. It was as if, on some primal level, I was transporting myself back nearly half a century to share my grandparents' pain.

Until I read my grandmother's diary, Theresienstadt had been a word I spoke almost sheepishly. "Yes," I would say, "my grandparents were Holocaust survivors. And they were interned in a concentration camp, but it was the 'paradise' ghetto … not so bad, not like the others." Once I knew their story, though, I felt guilt for having been their apologist.

I began to see my grandparents, at long last, through adult eyes rather than through the eyes of the child I had been. I had readily accepted assurances that everything was all right and, until I read the diary, had continued to believe that my grandfather was a kind and playful old man who was comfortable and at home in the world.

As I lay in bed that day, I began to see how terrified Opa must have been, living in a foreign country where he didn't speak the language. And even when he could converse, he had great difficulty hearing. I'd always known there was something not quite right about my grandfather's hearing because he wore an earplug with a wire that ran down his neck and into a bulging metal case in his breast pocket. Like magic, this shiny case enabled my grandfather to hear—though most of the time we still had to shout for him to understand. But, apart from his hearing, my grandfather seemed to me to be the perfect specimen of health and emotional stability. Because of what I would soon learn from my mother, however, I know otherwise.

Growing up, I had known nothing of the crying spells that came upon Opa almost out of nowhere like a summertime thunderstorm shatters the serenity of a peaceful sunset. Or of the old man sitting hunched over on the side of his bed in the morning, weeping uncontrollably, helpless to stand erect and begin a new day. The only grandfather I knew was the robust man looming over me whose broad smile and gleaming blue eyes always made me feel at ease and secure. How could I have known that he lived in fear of the slightest deviation from his everyday routine? That he relied on my grandmother to anchor his world?

And what of the frail woman with her upper left arm bloated from daily insulin injections? Though I was an adult when she died, I always thought of her as the woman hovering over me while I was growing up. Even in her last years, when she was strapped in a wheelchair so she wouldn't fall out, her head tottering toward one shoulder, I saw her as the precise and proper person she had always been.

I could never have imagined my grandmother's unfulfilled desires, fears and apprehensions, anger and rage. I knew nothing of her deep inner strength, without which she and Opa would not have survived Terezin. Or the terrible price she had to pay to save her husband. Or the hideous secret she carried all those years—not once seeking sympathy or to unburden herself. Of course I couldn't have known anything about these things she had never shared with anyone.

But when I read her diary, I knew. And I was overcome with remorse for wearing blinders, for accepting the easy answer that everything was fine. How could I, knowing that my grandparents had survived the Holocaust, have thought that was that? How could I have expected them to be like everyone else, like the grandparents of my friends? Children might accept things as they appear, but I was an adult. Of course no one told me, but I should have asked. And so I remained curled up in bed all that day and through the night. Not sleeping. Not eating.

And I faced some deeper truths, too. It was my grandparents, yes, but it was everything else in my life as well. I lived life from a distance, avoiding tumult and discomfort and sidestepping trouble. Why explore the depths when the surface is pleasant enough? Why look at suffering?

And what better example of this than Eve, the only woman with whom I had shared anything remotely resembling a relationship? I had witnessed all of her behaviors, but not once had I suspected the inner torment that stirred inside her. And when she finally divulged the horror that had haunted her for years I declined to share it, to feel it, or to help her. Instead, I withdrew. I stepped stealthily into a canoe and rowed away, backwards, my craft gliding slowly and silently on the surface of the deep and my oar dipping in only enough to carry me away.

But I behaved this way with everyone—clients, friends, and colleagues. I kept myself at a safe distance from all of them. No one knew me. I didn't even know myself. I lived the way I saw my mother, my grandparents, and other

Holocaust survivors I'd come into contact with, living. I saw that they were content to let life float by. The past was the past. Who could contemplate the future? Just accept the present for what it is and be grateful. But reading Oma's diary did more than help me to see this in myself. Through reading her diary, and meeting Feig, I began to understand that I needed to make a change.

Although I didn't realize it at the time, meeting Feig had begun to unsettle my comfortable distance from life. He required more of me than anyone ever had. His eyes held fast to mine like an anchor when I would rather have looked away. His raspy voice commanded my full attention as he told me things I did not want to hear. His vice-like grip clutched my forearm and would not let go until he was finished the conversation. He left me with no choice but to face life head-on.

The sun, hurling its first bright beam through a tiny opening between heavy gray clouds, brought me out of my torpor. Blinking in the fresh light, I climbed out of bed and made my way to the bathroom. A sudden surge of pressure against my penis reminded me that I hadn't even roused myself from bed to take a piss. I reached the toilet just in time. I shaved, showered, and dressed. I felt the familiar sensation of starting something new, but with one difference. The apprehension that I always carried within me on such occasions was gone. Instead, there was a hot sensation in my chest. Resolve had replaced fear. I was determined, and exactly what I was determined to do had begun to take shape.

First, I had to learn more about my grandparents. I'd loved them so dearly yet hardly knew them. There was only one person who could fill in the gaps for me, although I was far from certain she'd be willing. After all, she was my best role model for looking the other way. I cleared my calendar, put everything on hold, and booked a flight to Florida to visit my parents and convince my mother to open up—about her parents, the Holocaust, and herself.

• • •

My parents lived in a one-bedroom apartment in a high-rise condominium that, like its hotel neighbors the Eden Roc and Fontainebleau, had seen better days. But Miami Beach was on the mend and upbeat rumors abounded—including legalized gambling and real estate agents using pseudonyms for celebrity clients as they snapped up South Beach properties. Developers were converting rental buildings to condominiums, and older hotels and condominium buildings up and down the beach were refurbishing and putting on fancy faces.

"Goddamned condo fees keep going up!" my father complained when I called to tell him I was coming down. "And they want to put on a special assessment! What the hell do they know? I'm the one who was in real estate!"

I couldn't argue about that, and I didn't try.

"And the bastard speculators are buying small apartment houses in South Beach and kicking out the old people who've been living there for years," he went on. "It's a crime."

"Can they do that?"

"Not directly. They raise the rents so the old folks can't afford to renew. Most of these people live on social security."

"Where do they go?" I asked.

"That's the problem, son." I envisioned my father shrug at the other end of the line.

When I told him I was flying down the next day to visit, he was immediately suspicious. "Is everything all right? You're not sick or something, are you?"

"I'm fine, I just want to see you. What's so unusual about that?"

"Nothing. But you never visit without telling us weeks in advance. It's not like you. Can you leave your practice like this?"

"It's no problem. I'll only be staying a few days."

"David. I'm not stupid. What's wrong?"

"Nothing, really. I just want to get away for a bit. Actually, there's this woman—" I lied.

"So that's it!" My father snorted. "I knew it was something. Can't wait to see you!"

I looked forward to seeing him as well. Before he retired and my parents moved, we had lunch once a week. Just the two of us. I missed those times now that they were in Florida and enjoying the golden years which, they were recently reminding me, weren't as golden as they'd been made out to be.

The best thing about my parents' apartment was the stunning view. Every morning, they took their breakfast in the sunroom overlooking the white sands and tranquil blue Atlantic. Twelve months out of the year, my parents could watch people—strolling along the shoreline, relaxing in lounge chairs on the beach, or jogging on a raised flattened dune that merged onto a newly constructed boardwalk.

And this is what I loved best about Miami Beach. I'd get up early in the morning, strap on my Walkman, and head outside for a run on the boards. It was two miles to the northern tip of South Beach and two miles back with the sun, beach, and ocean always to one side. On my way back, I'd meet all sorts of people along the boardwalk—orthodox Jews, mostly women in ankle-length dresses walking briskly in white canvas sneakers; joggers and runners moving along at different speeds, bodies glistening and foreheads dripping in Miami's notorious humidity; and tourists who, sometimes two or more abreast, blocked the narrow path. Runners either slowed down and sidled past or shouted for them to move aside. I always sidled past.

Although there was a sofa bed in the living room, I never stayed at my parents' apartment. The sofa bed, I'd tell my mother, was too uncomfortable and my feet extended beyond the end. While this was true, it wasn't the real reason I took a hotel room a couple blocks away. The fact was, after having lived alone for so many years, I needed my own space. And my parents had their own routines that became even more inflexible as they grew older.

After my run and a shower, I'd join my parents for breakfast and a read through the *New York Times*, which my father would not replace with that "reactionary paper" the *Miami Herald*. Then, weather permitting, my dad would take his morning "swim," which meant a walk in the water. With bad sciatica and disintegrating discs he couldn't do much else, but his daily regimen in the water worked wonders and kept him going.

In the afternoon, he played pinochle with a group of men he called "the boys"—all of whom had been collecting social security longer than they cared to admit. Sometimes I'd come by for a swim to avoid the crowd at the hotel. I'd get a kick out of watching my father yell at his partner for missing a signal or curse the draw of the cards or flick his cigar ashes and overshoot the ashtray. It reminded me of the weekly card games he hosted at our house when I was growing up. The boisterous swearing and shouting of the four men seated around the kitchen table would keep me awake until they left—sometimes not until after midnight.

Then I'd look again at the elderly men at the card table, an awning protecting them from the blaring Miami sun. I'd squint, but there was no denying the old man my father had become—sparse thin tufts of white hair, mottled skin, sloping shoulders. Was I looking into a mirror of my own future?

My mother took her walk in the afternoons. Before the boardwalk was built, she walked on the bay side's promenade where boats and yachts were docked. Later in the afternoon she had a regular bridge game with a group of women, mostly widows.

Given their schedules, the only time I could be alone with my mother was in the morning while my father was in the pool.

"I didn't know you were seeing someone, David," my mother said. She was wrapping a leftover slice of lox and a sliver of cream cheese. She'd never allow anything to go to waste.

"I'm not."

"But your father told me it was girl troubles that brought you here. You wanted to get away, he said."

"Oh, yes." I had forgotten my lie. "But I really wasn't too involved."

"You should be, David. You're forty-one and I don't know what you're waiting for. A family is important, having children, and maybe even grandchildren—which is something your father and I are not likely to see." She slammed the refrigerator door and sighed. She planted herself with her hands on her hips and glared at me, her brown eyes burning.

"You're right about family being important," I said. She raised her eyebrows.

"In fact," I went on, "that's why I came and that's what I want to talk to you about. Can we sit in the sunroom?" She nodded and followed me into the glassed-in solarium facing the ocean. The bright sunlight reflected off the white marble floor in the only room with no heavy dark furniture.

She seated herself in the middle of a white wicker loveseat with lime and yellow cushions and I sat across from her on a matching rocking chair. The rocking motion reminded me of the swing set in our backyard and Opa pushing me with his broad hands. I was glad that he'd never pushed hard because I was afraid of going too high and falling. Even then, I avoided risks.

"Mom, I read Oma's diary. I wanted talk to you about it."

"I told you, David, I don't want to discuss it." Her slight shoulders stiffened and she straightened her back. "I'm just grateful that my parents lived through the War and made it to America. To see me married and then to see you born. To have a grandson. I thank God every night in my prayers for sparing my parents from being killed."

"How can you say that God saved Oma and Opa? And what if they'd died? Does that mean God would have been responsible for their deaths? If you believe that, then you have to say God is guilty of killing six million Jews and the millions of others murdered in the camps."

"I don't look at it that way. All I know is that my parents survived when the odds were against them. I thank God for—"

"Oh, cut it out!" I bolted from my chair and the rocker came close to tipping over. I had never raised my voice to either of my parents, and my mother's jaw dropped jaw and her eyes widened. But I couldn't help myself. I had come here seeking answers, and now I was being told that God was responsible for everything—the master puppeteer jerking the strings on mortal marionettes. "I can't believe you think God saved Oma and Opa. That's absurd!"

"Maybe, David, it would do you good to believe in God and go to synagogue. Then you might meet a nice Jewish girl. You know they have singles groups now at all the synagogues."

"Please don't change the subject," I said. I took a deep breath. I wasn't going to get sidetracked by some sort of ontological debate, although I could have told her that I did believe in God—just not the sort of supreme being who listens and responds to supplications from humans. I believed that God was the unifying force in the universe who could be experienced in a number of equally credible ways. It was organized religion that I abhorred. "You and I both know that God didn't save your parents. It was Oma who saved them."

My mother averted her eyes and slid down into the couch. She was not a tall woman. She'd never stood more than five foot two and now, due to some osteoporosis, she was no longer even that. If our argument became heated, or if she was forced to tell me what I wanted to know, she might sink into the couch and vanish altogether. But I wasn't about to let up.

"Are you saying that Oma never spoke about any of this? That she kept all that to herself? That Opa never knew?" She sat in silence. "I suppose not," I said.

"All right, let's move on," I continued. "We're the ones here today. We have to sort through the questions it all raises. Let's start with how you feel about it now that you know."

My mother stared at me, her face like granite. But there was a tear welling in the corner of her eye. Or at least I thought there was, and I began to wonder if I should be confronting her at all. Maybe I should have left well enough alone. But it was too late to put the blinders back on and I'd decided I wanted to change. I pressed on more gently. "We should share these feelings, Mom. It's so much better to get things off our chests than to keep them—"

"Better for who?" She broke her silence. The tear, if there had been one, was gone. She spoke in an icy, cutting voice.

"Well, better for everyone all around I should think." I sat down on the recliner.

"You want to know everything, David? You think my mother's diary says all there is to say? Who knows what else went on in that place? We don't have any idea. If that is what she wrote, can you begin to imagine what she couldn't write?" She leaned forward and evinced the sort of smile that elicited fear in my heart.

She was correct, of course. I'd never considered the possibility that my grandparents had been forced to endure more than what Oma had written in her journal. Once again, my blinders had served me well.

"Tell me, David, have you ever once thought about what was going on here while Oma and Opa assumed I was safe and out of harm's way? Any suggestions for what I should have said the day I met them at the docks? There I was, the daughter they hadn't seen for eight years, now a woman with a tall, handsome husband they had never met. Should I have unburdened myself? Should I have spoiled their joy in whatever years they had left? Should I have told them what I had to put up with in order to survive?"

My mother's cackle sent a shiver down my spine. It was as if Terezin's cold damp air had descended into the sunroom and was enveloping a new cadre of Jews—the progeny of its former prisoners. Maybe she was right. Maybe some things were best left unsaid. But even if I had wanted to end the conversation, I couldn't. Now that she had started, for the first time in her life my mother couldn't stop herself. She had bottled up her secret for so long that it came gushing out like molten lava from a long dormant volcano.

"The first thing my parents wanted, David, was to meet the couple who had sponsored me. They were just dying to fall on their knees and thank these angels from heaven who they believed had saved me from the Holocaust. But how could I do that?"

I shrugged. "Why not?" I asked. Had I missed something obvious?

My mother stared at me for a moment then let out a slight laugh before she went on. "I managed to put it off for years—always excuses. I never took Oma and Opa to visit these people who may have spared me from the gas chambers. But one day, out of the blue, they just dropped by our house.

"I didn't know what to say, David, and I don't remember exactly how I did introduce them. But I know what I would have liked to have said. Something like, 'Here everybody, I want you to meet Sir and Madame.' That's how I was instructed to address them. They always called me 'girl.' 'Oh here, girl, come here girl.'" She mimicked them in a stinging tone. She hesitated and took a deep breath but looked away from me as she continued.

"Sir was nice enough to work for, I suppose. Unless I failed to live up to his standards. The problem was, I could never be sure what his standards were. They varied. Like the way the wind changes before a storm. And then—

"The first time Sir hit me with his cane," she went on matter-of-factly, "the shock that he had dared to strike me stung more than the physical pain. My infraction? I didn't curtsey before leaving the room. I was halfway out the door when he struck me on my calf. I had a welt for a week. And Madame was no better, though she never beat me. She just slapped my face. And sent me to my room with no dinner if I behaved like 'a bad little girl.'"

I'm sure my face said it all. I was dumbfounded. "I never had the slightest idea," I finally said.

"You couldn't have known, David. I never let on. What purpose would it have served?"

"Couldn't you have left?"

"Where would I have gone? They were my sponsors. They threatened to send me back to Germany. And by then everyone knew what Germany was doing to its Jews. Of course, I found out much later that they were lying. If I had found other work I could have left them. But I didn't know that then. I was young and naive."

I felt the anger rise within me. I could have strangled Sir and Madame with my bare hands. But they were probably both dead, or not far from it.

I remember meeting them once. It must have been the visit my mother described, and I was five or six. They'd been in the neighborhood on a Sunday outing and they stopped by our house with their daughters. In those days, parents and children packed themselves into the family car and took a drive for the sheer enjoyment of it. And when people found themselves in a neighborhood that was home to people they knew, they dropped in to say hello.

I remember that I was playing in the yard when I heard my name called. I ran to the front porch where my parents and grandparents stood with a man and woman and two teenage girls whom I had never seen before.

The man wore a brown suit and brown felt hat. He was short, and his body was so contorted he reminded me of the "Rubber Man" at the carnival. When he leaned down to shake my hand, I smelled sweat from the moisture curdling around his tight white collar and there were beads of perspiration on his forehead. His nose looked like a hawk's beak and, somehow, I could tell that his smile wasn't real. He took my little hand in his and squeezed and wouldn't let go until I finally tugged so hard that it drew everyone's attention. Then he laughed and released me.

I also remember Madame. She stood with squared shoulders and, though it was a mild day, she wore a mink stole. I knew it was mink because my dad had bought one just like it for my mother, though she only wore it in cooler weather. Someone nudged me to say hello to her and Madame peered down at me over horn-rimmed glasses. She didn't smile or say a word but dismissed me with a nod of her head.

A sound of whimpering broke into my reminiscence. I looked up to see my mother's lips quivering and her face awash in tears. She made strange sobbing sounds—the result of her effort to keep the cries from escaping, on the one hand, and her desire to scream on the other. Intermittently, like the occasional crash of thunder, her cries cracked the silence between us.

I had wanted more than anything to talk with my mother about Oma and Opa. I wanted to know how she felt about the diary. I'd hoped she might tell me things about myself that I had forgotten or never known. I wanted to know how my father, a man born in America who knew nothing of the world from which my mother had come or of the horrors of the Holocaust, fit into all this. I wanted to talk about all this and more—for as long as her voice held out and I had the strength to continue asking.

But, in the end, there was only silence and nothing to say. Just my mother's soft shoulders shaking and me slipping onto the couch next to her and putting my arms around her and hugging her for the first time in a very long time. I heard her whisper through her sobbing that she loved me, and I heard myself say, through my own tears, that I loved her too.

I stayed for two more days. During that time, neither my mother nor I spoke a word about what had occurred that first morning. And yet everything had changed. It was as if there had been a barricade between us—like the ramparts of the fortress Terezin—and neither of us had had the wherewithal to surmount it or tear it down. Now, suddenly, it was gone.

This new openness between us made itself clear in subtle ways—a sparkling glint in her eyes, a repose in the corner of her mouth, a slight smile when she saw me enter a room. Though we both knew that we would not speak often, if ever again, of the Holocaust, or Theresienstadt, or the abuse she or my grandmother had endured, we also knew that we were no longer afraid to speak of these things. The load was easier to bear because we shouldered the millstone of that painful knowledge of the past together.

Neither of my parents was ready for me to fly back to Philadelphia, but I explained that I had things to do. "What can be so important you have to run back now? It's the weekend. You can go back Monday," my father told me.

"I have a client I have to see."

"And he can't wait?"

"No. Actually, he can't." I couldn't tell them that I couldn't wait either.

Many years earlier, I had made peace with my father and put away the kind of hurts that typically follow a father and son through adolescence and into adulthood. As I said goodbye to my parents, that day, though, I realized that only now had I truly come to terms with my mother—and she with me.

As the plane taxied down the runway I thought about the blinders that I'd left somewhere on the floor of my parents' sunroom at the foot of a rocker with lime and yellow cushions. The plane took off, bearing me into a new chapter of facing life head-on. It was time not just to be thinking about things or making plans or trying to reach decisions. It was time to take action, to bite into life without fear.

It was time to help Feig.

11

Back home, I spent the weekend catching up on paperwork and messages. Carol had called to see if I'd changed my mind about a plea agreement. I knew the drill—why prepare for a trial if a deal was at hand? There was also a message from Feig, his rasping voice thanking me profusely for posting bail. He promised I had nothing to fear concerning his appearance at trial and wanted to know what to expect next.

I didn't call either Carol or Feig when I arrived in my office Monday morning because I still didn't know what our strategy would be, though the beginning of a plan was beginning to take shape in my mind. But I did want to see Feig. I wanted to learn what happened after he was thrown on the train bound for Auschwitz. It was no longer a matter of idle curiosity.

So, on the way home that evening, I drove to Feig's house. When I returned his call that afternoon he'd said I could come by anytime. He even offered to cook dinner. Ilse had been ill for so long, he explained, that he had become quite the chef. Although I thanked him for the invitation, I begged off and stayed at the office until after the dinner hour had passed.

Street lamps and the neighbors' porch lights cast shadows over Feig's house. The bulb in the fixture by the side of his front door was flickering, so I lifted the bronze lid and reached inside to twist the bulb.

"Shit," I muttered as I yanked back my singed fingertips. I pulled a handkerchief from my pocket and turned the bulb until the fluttering ceased and a steady stream of light illuminated his patio.

Feig greeted me with open arms and a bear hug, and I buckled under his strength. He gave another squeeze and then withdrew to gaze into my face with a tight-lipped smile and moist eyes. I didn't know whether this display of affection was out of gratitude or because I was the only person in the world he could count on for help. Or perhaps it was because he was despondent and lonely or because he was happy to see a friend. By that time, I considered myself to be his friend—and he mine. I returned his smile. I was glad to see him as well.

"So good of you, David, so very, very good. What a *mensch* you are! Have you had dinner?"

"I grabbed a bite on the way over," I lied.

"How about some cake? Or coffee or tea?"

"Tea sounds good."

"Wonderful. This way." He spun on his heels and headed for the kitchen. There was a bounce in his step that I hadn't seen in a long time. It reminded me of the way his shoes used to click on the hallway at the Health Club, before his wife's stroke, when he'd come in for a workout and steam. If I were Feig, facing a criminal trial and a possible jail term, I don't know if I could have dragged myself out of bed in the morning. But he was a survivor, and giving up was against his nature.

Gazing into his blue eyes again reminded me of Opa, and I think my love for my grandfather just naturally spilled onto Feig. Although my desire to hear Feig's tale had almost everything to do with what I had learned about my grandparents, and my mother, over the past several days, there was also a very practical consideration. In order to best present his legal defense, I needed to know about his experiences during the Holocaust. And this would be the reason I'd give him for my questions about his time in Auschwitz.

Now, in hindsight, I see that part of what drew me to Feig's story was my desire to demand justice on behalf of the victims of the Holocaust—those alive as well as those kept alive by memory. Perhaps it was this moral outrage at the crimes committed against my people and my family that attracted me to the law in the first place. But I think that, more than anything else, it was my newfound desire to face life head-on, eyes wide open, that induced me to travel back to the most infamous death camp with Feig as my guide.

But none of this was clear to me that evening, when I was operating on overdrive with very little sleep. Dreams and nightmares that instantly escaped me had woken me every night since reading my grandmother's diary. My appetite had not returned, and I had even passed on one of Mrs. M.'s Shabbat dinners. It was as if my life was on hold until I fulfilled my charge with Feig—wherever that might lead.

So a good cup of hot tea was probably just the thing to calm my nerves as I sat down to hear what Feig would reveal.

He drank his tea just like Mrs. M., in the custom of Eastern European Jews of another time. He poured the tea into a glass and slowly sipped it through teeth clenching a sugar cube. I opted for the porcelain cup and added a squeeze of lemon. The tea was hot and warmed my insides.

Feig removed the sugar cube from his mouth and smiled. "So David, what is our strategy? What happens now?"

I settled into my chair and took another sip of tea before responding. "Jacob, there's something I want to talk about first. I'd like to hear what happened after you were thrown on the transport to Auschwitz."

"What does that have to do with my case?" His forehead furrowed in surprise, but his instantly darkened eyes sent another message. He was not pleased to discuss the subject.

"The fact that you're a Holocaust survivor may go to the heart of our defense, and I need to understand exactly what you went through before I can be more specific. Jacob, what happened after you found yourself in the cattle car?" He glared at me, but he knew he had no choice but to comply. With a heavy sigh, he continued his story. "I was in shock, David. My father had just died in my arms. I would see much of death after that, you know, but that was the first time I was so close to a dead body. I loved my father dearly." Feig's lips quivered. "When I came to my senses and realized where I was, I crouched in the dark and cried until I could cry no more."

"Did anyone come to your aid? To help you?"

"No," he said. "Why should they? Mine was not the only sound of suffering. There were many others, you know. A mother cradling her dead baby. A child whose leg was crushed in the stampede when the Jews were herded like wild beasts into the transport. The old man who was losing his mind because everyone he knew and everything he once had was gone. No, David. No one heard me. My cries evaporated into the air already thick with wailing. I was just one more instrument in the orchestra playing a requiem for dead souls."

Feig's tone was steady, but I had difficulty controlling the quaking in my own voice. "I can't imagine what it must have been like," I said. "I've read so much about the camps, the transports, the gas chambers, but—"

"That's right, David. You cannot begin to imagine." He stared into me, long and hard. He hadn't shaved for several days, and the stubble on his face that I had remembered as salt and pepper was almost entirely white.

"We had no room to move, you know," he continued. "If you fell, as I did after being shoved into the car, you might never get up. Families huddled together because, with so many people crammed so tightly, being separated for even a minute might mean eternity. It was so dark, you could barely see. During the day, we'd rotate by the barred window to breathe in the air and see the sky. Even if just for a moment, we could see there was still a world out there. Sometimes, we'd see green fields and trees and maybe the sky would be bright blue with white clouds, and we'd pass farms and villages and people going about their lives as if everything was normal. And for them it was almost normal. But inside, for us, the whole world had been turned upside down.

"Then there was the stench, David—that terrible stench. It was overwhelming. There was a waste pail in the corner, with a blanket hung for privacy, but the excrement spilled over because we could only empty the can when the train stopped and the doors were opened. But—" He sighed. "You got used to it."

"How did people manage without food?" I asked.

"Oh, there was food. That was the irony." Feig smirked. "Despite the rumors, almost everyone believed we were going to a work camp. To maintain this masquerade, the Nazis allowed the Jews to bring food on the transport. They even encouraged it, suggesting that a strong and well-fed body would get the better work assignments. And, in a way, that was correct.

"So people brought bread, cakes, hard-boiled eggs, fruit not yet ripe—foods that wouldn't spoil. Some even rationed their food, wanting to save it for when we reached our destination. If they only knew," he chortled, "they would have stuffed themselves!"

"But what did you have to eat? You had nothing with you."

"I managed." He shrugged. "Someone would give me a bit of crust, rotting fruit, whatever. I made do until the end of the line—Auschwitz/Birkenau."

I had read the words a thousand times. Through my tears, I saw them etched in the memorial at *Yad Vashem* in Israel. I heard them spoken by another survivor, the Nobel Laureate Elie Wiesel, but he was on a raised podium and I was seated twenty rows back, unable to see if his lips trembled or his eyes glistened with tears. But I was inches away from Feig, his eyes dry, his lips taut and drawn. He revealed nothing as he matter-of-factly described his arrival at Auschwitz.

"It was night, you know. But it was always night at Auschwitz. We never saw the sun. It hid behind dark clouds—clouds of Jewish ashes spewing from the crematoria into the sky. But when we reached Auschwitz it really was nighttime." He squinted into some faraway distance.

"The doors of the cattle cars were thrown open," he continued. "Madness followed—sheer madness. We tumbled onto the platform and were ordered into two lines—one for men and one for women. The air was filled with screaming and the barking of dogs snapping at our feet.

"Then came the selection. The selection, you know, meant life or death. I was very frightened. Unlike most of the others who had come from their homes or ghettos, I had been working hard labor and already looked like a skeleton. And after having very little to eat on the train, I was convinced I appeared too weak for work. An old man beside me took one look at me and must have thought the same thing. He leaned down and whispered into my ear that I should smack my face a few times to get the blood flowing to the cheeks to make me look healthy. So I did this.

"I was shaking as we filed past the table where he sat—the 'angel of death'—Mengele." Feig spat the name. "He leered at us like we were fish in a tank and he was deciding which ones to pluck and have for dinner. He had the darkest eyes I've ever seen. I'll never forget those eyes. I stood there long enough."

"Why was that?"

"You see, David, one's name had to be checked off the list. When I gave them my name, naturally it could not be found on the list of Jews who had boarded the transport. I was not supposed to be at Auschwitz. Wouldn't it have been nice if they had said a terrible mistake had been made and I was free to go!" He laughed. "But that is not what happened, of course. I presented a conundrum for the fastidious Germans. There was confusion. Why was I there? What to do with me? They screamed at me, wanting to know who I was and how I got there.

"I was much too terrified to speak. I just kept staring at Mengele. I couldn't take my eyes off of him. His face looked like it was carved from granite with a thicket of black eyebrows. Behind his thin lips I almost thought I saw the beginning of a smile—or was it the end of one?

"One minute, he looked at you as though he wanted to help and then suddenly, the next instant, he looked as though he was determined to heave you to the yelping dogs. The man was a contradiction, you know, and this is what was written on his face. Once he had been a healer—a man of medicine—but in Auschwitz he was a monster." Feig paused and gazed somewhere off my right shoulder.

In the silence, I wondered. Does a murderer lie buried within even the mildest of men? Is there a spark of kindness in even the vilest of criminals?

Feig sighed and went on. "The Germans who were arguing over the list gave up in frustration. The one holding the clipboard looked at Mengele. He wanted to know in which line he should place me. Mengele's eyes scoured my body. I felt as if I was being stripped naked. Those two or three seconds seemed like an eternity. Then I was shoved toward the line with women, children, and old men. I knew this meant death."

He leaned in so close that I could feel his breath on my face. His eyes locked on mine. He reached out to tap me on the knuckles. Then he grinned.

"But I'm alive, no?" He cackled. The creases disappeared from his face and his blue eyes lit up like a bright sky. It was as though he was about to tell me that this was the point at which he awoke from the nightmare. None of this had ever really happened, Auschwitz never existed, and the Holocaust was only a figment of someone's warped imagination.

"How did you?"

"There was this German officer, you know, standing behind Mengele. He was watching the whole episode with a look of amusement. As it turned out, he was in need of a houseboy and, somehow, I had struck his fancy. He whispered

something or other into the ear of a guard who came trudg-
ing after me and snatched me from the line of death I was
about to join. I didn't ask any questions or say a word. I knew
that wherever I was going had to be better than what awaited
me at the end of that line."

"And that's how you survived?"

"Yes. I was a houseboy for the duration of my time at
Auschwitz until the camp was liberated." Feig settled back.
His tale was finished. He told me what I had wanted to know.
"More tea?" he asked.

"No. No, thank you."

He rose and lumbered to the stove to pour himself
another glass of tea. He returned, slipped a sugar cube between his yellow teeth, and slowly sipped the hot tea. He set
down the glass and sighed, clearly relieved that the ordeal of
telling his tale was over.

But was it over? A few weeks earlier, I would have
been satisfied that his survivor's story had reached its conclusion. But something told me there was more. I stared into
his eyes searching for a sign and, suddenly, I knew there was
more. Much more. Feig's tale had only begun.

"I suppose being a house servant had its benefits," I
observed.

"What do you mean?"

"Well, like extra food, perhaps warm clothing, being
spared the selections."

He nodded, but he knitted his dense gray eyebrows.
He was growing wary.

"This officer—what did you say his name was?"

"I didn't."

"You remember, of course."

"Actually, we never were allowed to address him by his name. And now, after all these years, I don't recall any longer."

"What do you mean by 'we'? There were others?"

Feig nodded.

"Other houseboys like yourself?"

"Yes, David. There were others."

"How many?"

"Who knows?" He shrugged and sipped his tea. It was so quiet I could hear the tea sift through the sugar cube clamped between his teeth. He gulped, removed the sugar cube, and continued. "They came and they went. Some very quickly. Others lasted longer. One boy about my age had been there before I arrived and remained until the end."

"How was it determined who stayed and who went to the gas chamber?"

"That was up to Papa."

"Papa?"

Feig turned several shades of crimson. Then he let out a laugh that sent a chill through my bones. "Papa was the officer we served, David. That is how we were required to address him. Calling him anything else meant death, you know. And I don't mean the gas chamber. I saw Papa whip out his pistol and blow a boy's brains out—a lad no more than eight or nine—for calling him 'Sir.'"

He searched my face. I knew what he was thinking. This should do it. This should keep David from asking more questions. Who wants to hear of such things? Only a madman, and David is no madman. But he did not find the shock he was searching for in face. In a way, I had become mad— mad for the truth, whatever it was and wherever it led.

"Why did he insist on being addressed as Papa?" I asked.

"Why do you think?" Feig leaned closer. I could smell sweat and his acrid voice made my flesh crawl. There was something both sadistic and masochistic in his method. He was clearly intent on making me as uncomfortable as he could so I would stop asking questions. But, in order to try to make me stop, he had to open old wounds that would sear his soul all over again. He leaned back in his chair and slid his half-empty cup of tea over to one side. He folded his hands into a ball before him.

"We were instructed to call him Papa because he said we were his family. His 'little ones,' he liked to say. And you know, Papa liked to have fun with his little ones."

"What do you mean by 'fun'?" I forced myself to ask.

He stiffened. He hadn't meant to reveal anything about his life with "Papa" and the "little ones." It had slipped out. His false bravado and stern stare were gone. I looked into the eyes of a terrified boy and suspected that, if he told me anything more, it might be the first time he had spoken of it to anyone. "Jacob." I reached across the table and lightly touched the back of his hand. "What went on in that place?"

Feig's shoulders slumped and his pale face grew even more ashen. His lips trembled as he spoke. "Sometimes, you know, the wind shifted and brought the stench of charred flesh from the chimney stacks into our quarters. To make the smell go away, Papa drank himself into a stupor and then he'd order us to strip. He'd pull his penis out of his pants, swagger about dangling his prick in the air with its foreskin flapping, and proclaim how huge his penis was. He pulled and tugged at our pricks, making fun that they were circumcised and laughing at how small they were compared to his.

"Then, Papa commanded us to do things to each other while he'd sit in his huge chair drinking more schnapps and yanking away at his prick. One of two things always followed, David. Care to guess?" Feig's eyes blazed and a twisted grin crossed his face. He didn't wait for me to mumble a response but answered for me. "I didn't think so. If we were lucky—and imagine being lucky in Auschwitz!—Papa would fall asleep and snore until morning. But, most of the time, Papa would select one or two of us to have the honor of spending the night in his bed."

"Were you ever picked?"

He looked at me as though I had just asked him if the sun rose in the morning or if rain was wet. "Of course I was, David. How else would I have survived until the end?"

I was afraid to ask more. What right did I have? Additional information was unnecessary to the defense of his case. But I had to know. And, even more important, something inside me told me that Feig needed to tell more. Once he revealed everything, he would be better off.

"Jacob," I said as soothingly as I could. "What did he do to you? You have to get it off your chest."

He rose from his chair and leaned over the table. His fists were clenched and his knuckles were white. His nostrils flared like a bull charging a matador. Then, all at once, his entire body began to shake. His arms flailed. He ranted and raved, stomping around the tiny kitchen and crying out his answer through streaming tears.

To this day, I'm not exactly sure what he told me. It was bad. Worse than I would have thought or dared to imagine. His bellowing outburst thundered through the halls of his home and ricocheted off the walls. He never spoke of it again.

• • •

Driving home on that moonless night I was as un-nerved as I had ever been in my life. At the end of the beam from my headlights I saw Feig's face as he had looked at the end of his story, trembling and twisting like a wounded willow, battered and beaten by mighty winds yet refusing to yield ground. I saw myself standing up, hesitant at first and then determined, wrapping my quaking arms around him as his shoulders heaving into my chest. As though I could brace him against the storm.

If there were some way, perhaps by osmosis, that Feig's anguish could have been transferred to me, I would have received it gladly. Why? I'm certainly no glutton for punishment. But, at that moment, it was as if Feig were Opa, and all the torment and suffering that my grandparents had kept shut inside themselves until the day they died was com-ing out of Feig. And I had to have it. I needed to have it more than anything in the world if I was going to have the strength to face life head-on.

Feig and I exchanged no more words that night. We nodded. We grimaced. And, at the end, we even smiled with our faces awash with tears. We shook hands. We embraced. Our silence said everything.

12

The next morning I sat at my desk with my second cup of coffee, staring at the telephone, unable to dial Carol's number at the District Attorney's Office. As I watched my hand dart back and forth between my coffee cup and the phone, I remembered being a teenager and summoning the courage to ask a girl on a date. But my anxiety wasn't only about asking Carol to meet me for something more than the business at hand. My primary concern was what would happen if I couldn't obtain a plea bargain sparing Feig from prison. If that happened, I'd be forced to consider my backup plan. And that scared the hell out of me.

I called myself a coward, out loud, and phoned Carol. I took deep breaths as I listened to her answering machine and left a message for her to call me back so we could discuss Feig's case. Within minutes, she was on the phone.

"Screening your calls?" I asked.

"Nothing would get done if I didn't, David!" She laughed. "Things haven't changed since you were here— overworked, underpaid, and under-appreciated." She paused, waiting for me.

It was my phone call she was returning, and I was speechless.

"You said you were calling about your client, Mr. Feig?" she said.

"Yes," I said, "although that's not all. I did have something else in mind as well."

"Like what?"

"Well, how about the two of us getting together for dinner?" I realized I was sweating and wiped my forehead.

"Sounds good, David. The rest of this week doesn't work, but next week I can do—"

"What about Saturday?" I wanted her to know this was not merely a meeting to discuss a case, and a Saturday night would send that message.

"I'll have to get a sitter, but that should be no problem. Where do you suggest?"

"How about The White Dog? It's behind Penn's Law School."

"I know the place. Didn't we sometimes have lunch there?"

"I don't recall, but maybe we did." I knew very well that we did. "I'll get back to you on the time once I have reservations. Give me your address and I'll pick you up."

"No need," she said. "I'm totally out of your way. I'll meet you at seven unless I hear otherwise. And we'll talk about your client? I'd like to clear this file, David. No one wins in a case like this."

"We'll discuss it for sure." But she was wrong about no one winning. What was done was done. Ilse was dead. Feig stood accused of murder. And there was nothing I could do to change any of that. But the future was still up for grabs, and I was determined that Feig would come out on top. At least if my strategy worked. "The White Dog at seven, then. I'm looking forward to it."

"Me too."

The White Dog was situated on a narrow one-way street so I parked in a lot a few blocks away and walked. It was a pleasant evening and breathing the crisp fresh air calmed my nerves.

The place was packed with preppies, academicians, well-heeled patrons of the arts, and a few stylishly attired gay/lesbian couples. I spotted Carol at the bar and sidled through the crowd, trying to avoid bumping into one of the many self-absorbed individuals nonchalantly balancing a drink while affecting an air of consequence. Nothing had changed at The White Dog.

I always felt like an outsider among such people— people comfortable with themselves and their sense of belonging. I was the son of a first-generation American father and an immigrant mother and grew up in a home where German and Yiddish were spoken more than English. I felt like I was back at law school, intimidated in a crowd of Ivy League graduates with names reading like the Mayflower's registry. Which is why, despite the restaurant's great food and décor, I hadn't been back since my lunches with Carol.

Oddly enough, it was for this very reason that I'd suggested The White Dog. Things were changing. I was beginning to feel different about myself. I wanted to know what it felt like to swagger through this patrician crowd.

"Our table should be ready in a minute," Carol said above the din at the bar. I smiled and wedged myself between her and a thickset woman whose perfume made me feel like gagging.

"You look great," I said. She was perched on a stool with her legs crossed. I took in her thigh, revealed by her navy blue skirt, and her pale teal blouse open at the collar.

"You don't look so bad yourself," she said. The maitre d' called my name before I could order a drink. I took Carol by the hand and helped her down from the barstool, giving a not-so-innocent hip check to the fat woman with the repellent perfume.

The restaurant had been converted from several row houses and each room held four or five tables so that, once you got past the bar area, intimacy was the prevailing ambiance. We were led to a table for two in the corner of one of these rooms. We talked about the weather, her kids, and our work while perusing the menu.

Our waiter, a young man with a ponytail and pierced nose, proudly presented the bottle of Merlot I had ordered, cradling it like he was showing off a newborn swaddled in a blanket. He tilted the bottle under my nose and I nodded my approval. After committing our dinner order to memory, our server departed. He was obviously disappointed that we hadn't ordered appetizers. But why order an appetizer if a good enough house salad comes with the entree? That's what my mother always said. I would, however, depart from that and other habits in the weeks and months that followed.

"To a new beginning," I said, raising my glass in a toast.

"I'm not sure what you mean, David." Carol knitted her flaxen eyebrows.

"Neither am I, but that's the whole point of 'beginnings.' You're not supposed to be sure where you're heading." I smiled coyly and we clinked our glasses.

"David, back when we first met each other here at law school, were you attracted to me?"

I wasn't certain who was blushing more, but I saw crimson rise in her cheeks as I recognized the familiar tingling sensation across my own.

"You know the answer to that."

"Yes. I suppose I do. But why didn't you make a move? Because I was engaged?"

"Well," I said, "that certainly had something to do with it!" I laughed, easing the tension.

"But it's not like I was married and children were involved. Why did you let an engagement ring on my finger stop you? Was it because you weren't sure how I would respond?"

I finished my glass of wine. I topped up her glass and refilled mine.

"You knew I felt something, didn't you, David?" she asked.

I shrugged and smiled sheepishly.

"Then why?"

"It wasn't my nature to make waves."

"Yes, I suppose that describes you. You were always very cautious and thoughtful in control of yourself and everything around you."

"You make that sound like a compliment."

"It is."

"It shouldn't be. Look at the composed and risk-free life I've led and see where it's gotten me. I have a boring practice. I live alone. I do some writing, but it's mostly book reviews about other people's work and not my own." I stopped and took a healthy swig of wine. "But that's all about to change," I continued. "In fact, it already has." I looked into her sparkling eyes. A warmth filled my chest that had nothing to do with the wine.

"What do you mean that things are already changing?" She slid her hand across the table, gently brushing my own.

But I wasn't ready to answer her question. There was one thing that remained to be resolved before I could take Carol in my arms and show her what I meant by "beginnings."

As if on cue, our salads arrived, and when we were finished I turned the topic to Feig.

"Carol, I hate to bring this up but I have to. It's not why I asked you to dinner. I want you to know that. But I want to talk about it and get it behind us."

"You want to discuss your client, I suppose." I watched the subtle shift as she took on the professional demeanor of lawyer and prosecutor. She tightened her lips, narrowed her eyes, sat up a little straighter. She withdrew her hands from the top of the table.

"Yes, Feig," I said. "I would like you to reconsider a plea to assisted suicide with probation." She was about to object but, before she could, I continued. "Carol, I know how the game is played. Offers and counter-offers, back and forth, with everyone preparing for trial, and defense lawyers building their fees, and then a deal gets cut after a jury is selected. But, believe me, that is not going to happen here."

"You're still doing this *pro bono?*" she asked.

"That's not the point. Even if I'm not getting paid, I'll try this before a jury if that's what it takes. And if we're unsuccessful, I'll appeal. Whether I'm receiving a fee or not is irrelevant and has nothing to do with why I want to put an end to this."

Although I didn't mean to, I had spoken loudly enough to attract the craning necks of a foursome at the next table. Carol's eyebrows rose and she blushed. She was clearly taken back by my mild outburst.

"I meant it as a compliment, David, about you not charging a fee," she said soothingly. "With all the lawyers I see plea bargaining with their clients' lives or going to trial unprepared, I admire you for being so devoted to Mr. Feig."

She returned her hands to the table and slowly slid them in my direction. They stopped barely an inch from my own hands, and it felt as though a mild jolt of electricity flowed from her fingertips to mine.

"I know. I'm sorry. But I'm a bit sensitive about this case."

"You certainly are!" Carol laughed and the strain between us abated. "Is it because your client is a survivor?"

"Yes, but it's more than that."

"You can't let that get in the way of your professionalism. You have to remain objective if you want to give your client the best representation possible. But then, I'm not telling you anything you don't already know." She smiled.

For that instant, I wished I had never met Feig. I wished I could just be here with Carol, not discussing this case. But Feig had become a part of my life and, if he hadn't, I wouldn't have been having dinner with her in the first place.

"It's not that simple. Sometimes, a passionate defense is called for."

"Is that what you have in mind?"

"If it goes to trial, yes."

Carol stared directly into my eyes, seeking what I was shielding. Then she sat back and sighed. I could see the game was up. She was going to capitulate and give me her best offer now and not drag it out for months. I could see it in the glitter that returned to her green eyes.

"You drive a hard bargain, Mr. Gold." She smiled. "I can take assisted suicide."

"Great," I said.

"But there has to be some time served."

My heart sank. "I can't accept that, Carol." Her eyebrows arched, revealing her genuine surprise. The offer was more than reasonable, and here I was turning it down out of hand. "I'm sorry, but I made it quite clear that my client is not going to prison. He'll do community service, take probation for as long as you want, even house arrest. But no jail time."

Carol looked at me as if I were mad—as if the man seated across the table from her was not the same person she had once known. She'd known the David Gold who had always taken the conservative and safe road, who would have listened to reason and accepted the certainty of a sound plea agreement. "David, I'm being more than fair."

"I know that."

"You're not being reasonable."

"Maybe not."

"I can't do better. This comes from my boss. The case is attracting more than its share of publicity. We've received calls from fringe groups and even respectable organizations insisting we uphold the sanctity of life. And you don't even want to know about the weekly messages the deceased's children are leaving for me, calling your client an out-and-out murderer. There just has to be some time served." She was pleading. She leaned over the table and reached out her arm.

"I'm really, really sorry, Carol. We'll just have to go to trial." My back stiffened.

Our entrees arrived and, other than small talk, we ate in silence. I finished the Merlot. We passed on dessert and, after paying the check, I politely asked her if she wanted to go to the bar for an after-dinner drink. She declined. The damage was done. There was a sadness in her eyes and the sparkle was gone. But I was determined to bring it back—just as soon as I could spirit Feig out of harm's way and ensure that he was safe.

13

"Hello, David," Feig said as he opened the door to his home. I could tell from the way his forehead furrowed that he was concerned about my wanting to see him right away. "Come in, come in."

The house reeked of oldness, of the way old people and their clothing smell when they don't care anymore. It's a staleness that reminds me of camphor drifting out of a can of mothballs tucked away in the corner of a cedar closet preserving apparel so ancient it would have been better discarded.

As we walked past the plastic-covered sofa and chairs in the living room, the stench of leftover food wafted in from the kitchen. I envisioned the piled remains waiting to be stuffed down the garbage disposal. Feig's musty sweater draped his frail frame as if he were no more than a clothes hanger. He lowered himself slowly into a chair at the dining room table and pulled out the chair next to him for me.

"Is there something I can get you, David," he said wearily.

"No, thank you." I fidgeted, not sure how to begin.

"So, this must be important, no?"

"It is."

"Then get it off your chest," he said.

Although I'd rehearsed what I would say to him on the drive over, now that I was sitting next to him I couldn't find the words.

"It's about my case, isn't it?" he asked.

I nodded.

"Is it bad?"

"Yes and no," I said. "But first, there's something I need to know."

"What is it?"

"You met your wife in Israel, didn't you?" I asked. The question startled him. I watched the glimmer in his eyes as the memory stirred. Once he'd been a young man with a living and vibrant wife. "Yes, we met in Israel. It was Ilse's first trip after her husband died. But she didn't travel alone. She was on a tour with Hadassah. Ilse was very big in Hadassah, you know." He beamed. "She was chapter president, and their visit to the Hadassah Hospital in Jerusalem was the highlight of the journey."

"How did you wind up in Israel, Jacob?" I asked. As he slunk down in his chair, I remembered how he had looked that first time I met him in the steam room at the Health Club. I'd been so impressed with the quiet strength and dignity he exuded, with how his graying hair bespoke a wisdom that comes with experience, with how his age was not a handicap that cursed him but rather a source of knowledge. Feig hadn't been at the club at all since he was arrested. Although I was determined to make changes in my life, I remained at the Health Club. I felt comfortable there, and comfort was something I still valued.

I also had an aptitude for patience, so I sat and waited for him to respond to my question. I knew this was not easy for him—and that what would follow would be even more difficult.

Finally, exhaling deeply, he began. "The end at Auschwitz came in the middle of January 1945. Shouting and floodlights and dogs barking woke me in the night. It reminded me of the night I had arrived." Feig squinted, as if peering down a bleak tunnel of dark memory. "We had heard rumors the Russians were not far," he went on, "and we were afraid the Germans would kill us all rather than leave even one witness. So, I thought to myself, this must be it—the end had come.

"From where I had been sleeping on the floor I saw Papa, drunk as usual, stumbling about in a stupor. He grabbed what he could and then bolted out the door. Without even a goodbye, he left us!" He flashed a wry grin. "Me and another boy about my age were all that remained of Papa's 'harem,'" he snickered. "We peeked out the window. Every barrack was being emptied. Thousands of people for as far as we could see were standing in the freezing air, shaking with cold, while the Germans spent hours taking roll call. When this was finally done, everyone began to move out to begin the long march to Germany. The other boy—what was his name?" Feig asked himself, scratching his stubbled chin. He finally gave up and continued with a shrug. "Well, me and this boy, we both thought that we'd managed to avoid the march when the front door burst open and a German guard—a lad not much older than we were—barged into the room. I'm not sure if he was more surprised or afraid or if we were—but I think he was just looking for some loot or food, you know, and here instead he found two half-naked boys staring back at him. David, he lifted his rifle and I thought he was going to shoot us on the spot. He began waving it back and forth and mumbled something that I couldn't hear. But as he gathered his courage—after all, he was the one with the weapon—he started to shout *'Raus Juden! Raus Juden! Macht schnell!'* That much I understood all too well. We each grabbed a jacket and ran out of Papa's quarters as fast as we could with the young Nazi on our heels. We didn't stop until we caught up with one of the last contingents to depart from Auschwitz."

Feig took a breath and his eyes met mine. "Perhaps this answers your question?" his look seemed to ask. "Enough? You want to hear more?" He remained silent, waiting for me to acknowledge the end of his story. Out of Auschwitz. To Israel. The miracle of a survivor. It is enough.

"And then what?" I asked.

His frown and arched eyebrows reflected both disappointment and surprise. Darkness shrouded his eyes as he continued. "We walked. Or, should I say, we slogged, we shuffled, we even crawled on all fours like animals. West ... towards Germany. You know of these 'death marches,' no?" Feig knew that I knew, but I nodded anyway. "So," he said, "I need not tell you how one day was just like every other. I don't think any of us had ever been so cold. Frozen to the bones so they ached all the time—even when we slept. Swollen feet. Bloody feet. Frostbitten feet, hands, fingers, noses, and cheeks. Hunger that would drive a man to eat another man's corpse and sometimes, you know, sometimes one did." He said it without judgment, as though he were describing the weather.

"So many bodies falling," he went on, "in front, in back, to the side. Sometimes a body fell from exhaustion. Sometimes a body fell because it was shot. Sometimes a body fell from exhaustion and then it was shot.

"At night, if we were lucky, the German officers commandeered houses for themselves and assigned the kapos and guards to take us to sheds or barns. If not for that, we all would have died. But those nights, a respite from that arctic hell, sustained some of us. Sometimes there was even food to be had. Of course, you had to catch and kill it first—a chicken or pig or a dog or a cat."

He paused and his burning blue eyes bored through me. He was waiting for me to yield. But I held my ground. As horrible as these things were, he hadn't yet said anything I hadn't expected. His story was similar to that of every survivor and every victim. It was what went on inside a person that was unique. That was what I needed to know. I believed we were at the point at which Feig could no longer contain what he had bottled up for so long. He'd reached the place in his narrative where he had to talk not just about what he'd observed, but about how he felt. Reluctantly, he continued on a different tack. In a way, he was beginning to surrender himself.

"Until the death march, you know, I had never seen death except for my father and the boy whose brains Papa blew out. Imagine that! I spend almost a year in Auschwitz and had not seen people die! How is that possible, David?" He snorted. Then his face grew ashen and his eyes dull. "But on the march, you know, death was all around me. The boy who was with me in Papa's house did not last the first week. He was shot not two seconds after he fell. Someone ripped off his shoes. Another took his pants. I took his jacket and put it over mine. One of the dogs started tearing away at his naked flesh."

A wave of nausea spread over me, but I forced myself to stare at him, bidding him to go on.

"It affects the soul, you know."

I shook my head slightly, perplexed.

"Allow me to explain, my friend. Allow me to tell you what happened to the adolescent known as Jacob Feig."

And then the tale began—the one I had been waiting all this time to hear.

157

"I was once happy, you know. Growing up in Sighet. We knew who we were and who we weren't. The world made sense, and when it did not, God had a reason, whether we understood it or not, and we accepted that. We were not rich but we had food and shelter and clothes. We celebrated our holidays and birthdays and observed Shabbat once a week. What more was there?

"Then came 1944, and the world turned on its head. It was hard to comprehend, let alone accept. But I did. I accepted being exiled from my home—from Sighet. Unable to return. My father shot. Thrown on the cattle car. The stench. The hunger. The sordidness of Papa. God has His reasons, I would remind myself. God has His ways. We must accede to this. This I had been taught. And so I held onto my faith. Onto my soul.

"But the march? No, this was something I could not accept. It was beyond the power of any mortal, let alone a fourteen-year-old boy, to comprehend. Day in and day out, death and dying, murder and killing.

"You know, David, every night of my life, for as long as I could remember, I used to whisper the Shema just before going to sleep, declaring my belief in God. And then, one night during the march, I could no longer utter the words that had always come so easily. They stuck in my throat and I gagged on them as one would choke on pork.

"So instead of reciting the Shema while trying to go to sleep, I started to ask God questions. Why do You allow this to happen? What kind of world is this where there is no justice? Where the murderers prevail. Where good people are the victims and the evil ones are victorious. For what purpose? Towards what end?" Feig extended his arm and tapped his talon-like fingers on the back of my hand and smiled a hellish smile.

"And what did God have to say to all this? What words of wisdom or assurance came forth from the Almighty? Did Yahweh say anything to comfort an adolescent who was about to lose his soul? No. God said nothing. The omnipotent Jehovah was silent. Silent, David. Silent as a stone."

I was not surprised by his questioning of God or God's silence. Only a few were able to hold onto their faith in God despite the horrors going on around them. But Feig's reaction to this silence, as I was about to learn, was something altogether different. And, as his tale unfolded further, it sent a chill coursing through my veins.

"So, what did I do, David?" He leaned back in his chair and grinned. "I gave as good as I got! Even better! If God was going to remain silent, then what could be more appropriate than to follow His example. I swore that I, too, would be silent! No more prayers or supplications or questions directed to the Almighty. But why stop there? If it was good enough for God not to speak to his people, the ones who were dropping and dying all around me every day—some with devoted prayers on their lips—then I would be silent with them as well. No more talking. Not even a whisper. I vowed an oath to be silent for the rest of my life—however brief that life might be."

An eerie sensation was germinating in the pit of my stomach. Wild thoughts, like bats bouncing off dark cavernous walls, flew through my mind. But it was too farfetched a notion, so I said nothing and waited for Feig to continue.

"But here I am, David, babbling on and on. Obviously I did not stick to my vow." He laughed and a glint returned to his eyes. "But in fact I did not speak for quite some time—months, in fact. Not a word passed my lips throughout the remaining weeks of the march. I didn't utter a sound when, near the end of the march, with spring in the air and the flowers beginning to bud, when it was least expected and when we thought the worst was over—we were struck by a snowstorm.

"Such a storm, David," Feig said as he shook his head. "The snow was so thick we were blinded and wandered about like mice in a maze. It stopped as abruptly as it had come, and when we saw the bright sun in a clear sky again—there we stood, about fifty of us guarded only by that young German soldier, the one who had found me in Papa's house. The rest of the march was nowhere in sight."

"Did you overpower the soldier? Escape?" I asked. He frowned. "No, we did not. And why should we? Even after he would have emptied his rifle into us, even after those left standing had torn him limb from limb, then where were we to go? We had no idea. This young man sensed this. He was not stupid. He told us he would take us to a camp he had heard of where Jews were not murdered. He studied a map. It was not very far, he said, maybe a week's march. Maybe we could survive the War at that place, he said. We looked around us. Only emptiness and snow in every direction. At least if we remained with the soldier, he might commandeer some food or shelter. He had authority. He had a gun. He offered us hope. So we followed him like a herd of cows.

"The Kraut was right, you know. It was a week's march. Had it been two, we all would have been dead, because two or three of us dropped every day or didn't wake up from the sleep we fell into the night before." The furrow in his forehead revealed that there was something he was trying to recall and, when he did, he smiled.

"You know, David, it was like a fairy tale. At the end of the day's march, with the sun setting, we saw a castle in the distance. It was a fortress, as it turned out, and as we approached I imagined there would be a king and queen there—a Jewish king and queen—a King David or Queen Esther. And I would be fed until my belly would burst and I'd be given blankets and a bed to sleep in where I could wake up on my own, and not because there were dogs barking or the butt of a rifle striking me or Papa kicking me with his boot." Feig frowned.

"It was a castle all right," he continued, "but there was no Jewish king or queen. It was just as the German soldier had told us—a camp for Jews where there was no gas chamber. But Jews died every day there from hunger, disease, and the hangman's noose. Can you believe that, David! A castle the Nazis made for the Jews!"

"Yes!" I wanted to shout. "Theresienstadt! I know it. My grandparents were there. I told you that when we first met. Don't you remember, Jacob? And did you keep your silence there as well? Or did you speak once you passed through the fortresses' gates? Were you the quiet one whose lips remained shut? The one who Oma ..." But it was my turn to choose silence. Feig had to finish his tale before we could move on to the story it appeared we shared, implausible as it seemed.

"Naturally," he continued, "it was not a castle built for Jews but a fortress named after the Austrian Empress Theresa before that area became part of Czechoslovakia. Can you believe it, David? We made it all the way from Poland to

Czechoslovakia. Not bad for a boy who, only a year before, had never ventured more than a few miles from the mountain village where he had lived his whole life." Feig laughed. But, seeing that I did not share his sense of irony—a device, I concluded, he employed to shield a myriad of buried emotions—he continued. "Anyway, we were marched to the German headquarters where our Aryan Moses left us to stand in the cold while he argued with a German officer about whose responsibility we were. No one seemed to want us. Once they disappeared into the building—where, no doubt, it was warm—a small delegation of Jews appeared and scurried us away for fear the Germans might decide to shoot us. After all, we were not 'privileged' Jews entitled to reside in the lovely village the Germans had so graciously provided." Feig spat these last words.

"You mean you went off with everyone else?" I asked. I was beginning to think that I'd jumped to a hasty conclusion, and a wave of disappointment surprised me.

"Of course I did. What do you think, David? That I remained standing, alone, to starve to death? That I had given up and wanted to die? That I no longer cared about anybody or anything because everyone I loved was gone and there was nothing and no one to return to? So why not just stand there and wait for a bullet to put an end to my life? Or freeze to death? Or fade away as if I had never existed?"

I looked into his eyes and watched sorrow replace the anger that had been there only moments before. He had lost his mother, sister, and father. His life had been stolen from him. He had endured unimaginable pain and witnessed unimaginable horrors. "Yes, Jacob," I said. "That is exactly how you felt and why, I believe, you simply stood there in the cold that day and didn't follow the rest of your group."

I'd seen the look on Feig's face before. More than a few of my clients had made up a story, fabricated a lie, and ultimately came to believe it was true. But, as I waited, I saw uncertainty and then realization gradually sweep across his face. No, he said, that's right, he did not go with the others. He told me that just as he had chosen silence, he had chosen death—to remain outside the German headquarters in Theresienstadt where he would be allowed to die.

"But Jacob, you did not die," I said. "So what happened?" I knew then, without a doubt, what would follow. When Feig sighed deeply, he expelled more than air. Something that he had kept within him for his entire adult life escaped at that moment. It was as if someone had broken into an Egyptian tomb that had not seen the light of day for millennia, and the stale acrid air struck me in the face.

"My feet wouldn't budge, you know. I wanted them to, but they wouldn't. I did not have the energy or the will to take one more step. So, I remained to die." His lips trembled and tears welled in his eyes. "And then, the most amazing thing happened. As if dropped from the sky, a woman appeared. Middle aged, maybe older, it was hard to tell under the circumstances. In a way, despite everything, she was beautiful. She had black hair with streaks of gray, dark eyes, and high cheekbones. She was not a big woman but she took small but determined steps toward me. She fixed her eyes onto mine and would not let go. It was as if she read what my eyes said when even I was unaware of what they were communicating anymore.

"When she reached me, she said something in German that I did not understand. She waited for an answer. Then she asked for my name. That much I understood, and I tried to tell her, but my oath of silence had cemented my lips shut. It was as if I had forgotten how to talk. She studied me, smiled, and took me by the hand. My feet shuffled along beside her as though they existed apart from me. I was not going to die. My time was not up. This woman saw to that."

"Did this woman have a name?" I asked. My heart pounded.

Feig gazed at me as if I had asked the most absurd question for which, despite its insipidness, he had no answer. He shrugged apologetically. "You know, David, I don't know. I never spoke to her, or to her husband, who was as kind as anyone could be under the circumstances. They welcomed me into the tiny sparse space they had to themselves. They even shared their rations with me since, officially, I did not exist. But I never had the need to address her, so if she did tell me her name I must have forgotten.

"But this woman was like an angel sent from God—a god in whom I no longer believed. But as the days and weeks passed and death no longer confronted me at every corner, I began to return to the land of the living. I gained weight because, despite the meager rations, it was more food than I had been accustomed to. I also began to sleep the kind of normal sleep where dreams are dreamt instead of nightmares. In time, I even became less angry. I came to believe that there were still some people who retained their humanity and ability to be kind to others even in the worst circumstances.

"Gradually, David, through the compassion of this woman, I began to hope that I did have a place in the world and, more important, a future. I forgave the victims who did whatever they had to do to survive. I forgave the rest of the world that did not come to our aid. But the Nazi murderers and their henchmen, I did not forgive. Why should I?" Feig's eyebrows arched in defiance. "And you know who else I did not forgive, David?"

I shook my head.

"I did not forgive God, that's who! I did not forgive God, and I have not forgiven God to this day for what He allowed to happen."

"Perhaps," I suggested, "it is not God but Man whom you should hold accountable and not forgive."

"No." He shook his head and thumped his fist on the table. "It was God's work!"

"I don't want to get into an ontological debate with you, Jacob, but maybe, just maybe, God had nothing to do with it. Perhaps it was the work of humans and God could not interfere." I wanted to add that his thinking was just as infantile as that of my mother thanking God for sparing her parents when it was chance or fate or their own actions or some combination of all of those that kept Oma and Opa alive. Both Jacob and my mother were wrong to assign omnipotence to God.

"Then, David, if what you say is so, God would not be God." He said this matter-of-factly and folded his arms across his chest.

Knowing that his thinking wasn't about to change, and anxious to make this connection between us that I still hardly believed could be true, I decided not to continue to challenge him about the anthropomorphic deity whom he held responsible for the Holocaust.

"All right then," I said. "You did not forgive God. So what happened next?"

The corners of his mouth twitched as he chalked up a modest victory in our sophistic disputation. Then he continued. "As I said, David, I did forgive mankind—at least some of them. And, by the time Theresienstadt was liberated, I had resolved to give up my vow of silence."

"You mean you decided to speak again? Before you left the camp?"

He nodded. But my grandmother wrote that she never heard the boy speak, not even when they parted. "You spoke before you left Theresienstadt? To this woman?"

Feig looked as though he had been struck in the face. Tears welled in his eyes once more. "No, David I remained silent. I meant to speak to her. To thank her for restoring my life. For letting me believe once again that humans can be good to each other. But I did no such thing." He shook his head wearily and looked down at his feet. "I did not, could not, say goodbye to her, David. So when we were separated on the day of liberation, I shuffled off and never saw her again. I'll take this with me to my grave. It is the one thing that I'll always regret and that I cannot do anything about. I never thanked her." His shoulders slumped and he folded into himself.

I stood up and placed a hand on Feig's shoulder. I looked down and smiled. "You can thank her grandson, Jacob," I said.

He looked up at me, not comprehending. But then, slowly, recognition began to light up his face. The story about my grandparents that was the topic of our first conversation. Yes, they ended up at Theresienstadt and yes, they did survive. Still, he was not convinced until I told him about my grandmother's diary and what she had written about the silent boy she had taken in.

Feig collapsed and cried as a beast unburdened of a great yoke. He rose and grabbed me in his arms. We cried and talked some more. The healing had begun. For both of us.

14

Had the resolution of Feig's past and the recounting of the final chapter of his story been all there was to accomplish that night, I would have taken my leave, driven home, and fallen into a deep and tranquil sleep. But that was only part of the reason I had come to see him that evening. There was also the matter of the present and, even more, the question of his future.

And so I remained with him. Once the emotionally charged revelation of the incredible story we shared had begun to settle in, we fell back into our chairs and all was quiet for a time. He finally broke the silence.

"Do you want a drink, David?" he asked as he lifted himself from his chair. "Some schnapps?" I shook my head. Feig trudged to the kitchen cabinet, removed a bottle of Scotch, poured himself a shot, and returned to the table.

"I suppose you still want to know how I ended up in *Eretz Yisrael*," he said. "Well, you certainly are entitled to know, my friend—perhaps more than anyone else. It was a roundabout route, that's for sure." He grinned.

"After the liberation of Terezin, I was shuttled from one DP camp to another—none of them much different from Auschwitz except the food was better and we weren't shot at or sent to gas chambers. Finally, I was transferred to an HIAS orphanage where I completed my education. That's where I learned English and Hebrew. When I was old enough, I remained as a counselor for the younger children until the time came for me to be sent to Israel. This was in 1949, after the War of Independence. Before then, there was no place to go—no country willing to take me in other than Hungary, and I wasn't going back there."

"So you became an Israeli citizen?"

"Yes, of course. Every Jew has that option, you know."

"The Law of Return."

"That's right. But it was too late for so many." Feig's face darkened. He glared into his glass, then smirked and raised a toast. "Here's to you, Papa!" he bellowed. "You son-of-a-bitch!" He downed the Scotch. "I've always wanted to do that, David. And now I have!"

I knew I needed to reveal my plan to him, and I was beginning to regret having passed on the Scotch to fortify myself. "Jacob," I began, "I met with the assistant district attorney assigned to your case." I saw no reason to add that our meeting was over dinner or that discussing his situation had spoiled the evening.

"You mean that pretty lady at the hearing?" Feig asked. He still had a fine eye for women.

I nodded. "Jacob, listen carefully. There is a deal on the table and it's the best we'll get." His bristly eyebrows gathered and he leaned forward. My voice was barely above a whisper, but I spoke clearly and slowly.

"What do you mean by a 'deal'?" he asked.

"They're actually called 'plea agreements.' The prosecutor and defendant agree to a guilty plea in exchange for a sentence recommendation that the judge usually follows."

"You mean I must say that I murdered Ilse? I did not do this." He fell back in his chair, his eyes wide with shock. "Is this what you suggest, David?"

"No." I reached out and patted his forearm and offered the assurance of a weak smile. "First of all, the offer allows you to plead to assisted suicide and the murder count is dropped."

"Well, actually David, that is what happened, you know."

"True. But here's the problem. The prosecutor insists you serve some time in jail."

Feig's cheeks flushed red and his teeth clenched in panic and rage. His nostrils flared. "No!" he thundered as he smashed his fist on the table. "I won't let them have me again! I'll not be caged behind bars or barbed wire or barrack walls. The *goyim* will not have me again! Do you understand, David?" Now he was roaring.

"Yes, yes, I know that, Jacob. They won't have you again."

"You must get them to agree to this, David."

"It's the best deal they're going to offer, Jacob. But I told them it wasn't good enough."

"So what are you saying? That there will be a trial?" I could see his thoughts. Suppose he was found guilty? What would happen if he were? How could he survive prison?

"This is what we must discuss, Jacob." I spoke evenly and carefully, trying to maintain an air of confidence. I had learned over the years that clients need to hear from their attorneys how things will play out—regardless of the result. The problem is that lawyers seldom know any more than anyone else about what the outcome will be, and especially when a jury is involved.

Nonetheless, I was certain of my plan. I slowly disclosed it to Feig and, although at first he stared at me wide-eyed, as if I were mad, I watched the tension in his body ease as I went on.

And, indeed, some would have thought me mad. After my scheme was executed, those who learned how it hatched considered me more than mad. But Feig had confidence in me. He knew that my only concern was his welfare.

All I wanted, regardless of the risk and cost to myself, was to spare Feig from prison—and my plan would accomplish that.

When I was finished, Feig had many questions. I fielded them all with the aplomb of a man convinced of the rightness of his purpose and design. While he asked and I answered, he made us tea and poured more than a splash of schnapps into our cups. The warm brew invigorated me and, despite the late hour and a general weariness, I answered each of his questions until he was fully satisfied that my strategy was sound.

"Well, David," he sighed as he gathered our cups and saucers, "I truly don't know how to thank you—or if I can ever repay you."

"No need for either," I said as I rose from my chair.

"We may never see each other again once this is over, you know."

Tiny tears were trickling down his cheeks and, as I felt the welling in my own eyes, I knew the time had come to leave.

I drove home that night without a thought in my head. Some say that's impossible, that a person always has to be thinking of something. But my mind was blank. I drove home by rote, went right to bed, and fell asleep instantly. I slept soundly, the way a man who has found peace sleeps. The way a man sleeps when he knows he has cast off a lifelong burden and that, when he wakes, he will begin the day free from past constraints. Not only had I resolved to take action—I had decided to do something I had never dreamt of doing.

That is how I slept. That is how I woke. That is how I remained in the days that followed, and particularly on the morning I went to pick up Feig.

It was a Sunday, and so early that the sun was just beginning to rise on the horizon. The roads were almost deserted and the sidewalks were empty except for a few families scurrying to the first Mass of the day.

For a while we drove in silence. Feig's features reminded me of a statue, firm and hard, but with eyes soft and fragile. His posture was erect, like a military officer on his way to lead his troops into battle.

As we drove, Feig took in his final glimpses of the city he had come to call home. He would never see Philadelphia again. This was not the first time he was forced to flee, but I hoped it would be the last.

I pulled into short-term parking. I wouldn't be gone long, assuming the plane was on time. When I had called before leaving home, it had been right on schedule. Not that EL AL was known for its punctuality, or fine food, or courteous flight attendants, or anything besides its security, which was the best in the world. It had to be.

Over Feig's protest, I lugged his suitcase and left him to strap his carry-on over his shoulder. The international terminal was a beehive of activity. The EL AL desk was tucked away in a corner of the terminal, and the line was already jammed with those who would be accompanying Feig on his journey home. EL AL had only one flight from Philadelphia to Tel Aviv. Other flights were available by shuttle to JFK in New York, but I preferred the direct route. The fewer check-ins the better.

Feig and I joined the end of the line, which was made up almost entirely of Jews. There were the "black hats"— bearded orthodox men in black felt hats with *tzitzit* spilling over dark wrinkled trousers. Women with scarves on their heads hovered over broods of children, some dressed in clothes too big or too small—obvious hand-me-downs from siblings. There was a large multi-generational family group that included a fidgety gaunt boy probably destined to have a bar mitzvah at the Wailing Wall. A striking olive-skinned brunette with a fine figure slung her arm over a young man about her age and I took them to be *sabras*, native Israelis.

Except for a group of priests and a family with a young girl wearing a crucifix, it seemed that all of Feig's fellow travelers were Jews. There's this thing about one Jew being able to sense the presence of another. Nothing need be spoken, no reason or rationale. You just knew. Over the years, I had become convinced it was something in the genes or bloodline. But whatever it was, it was there.

When we reached the front of the line, Feig placed his tickets and photo ID on the counter. The EL AL agent, a middle-aged woman with pronounced cheekbones and auburn hair drawn taught in a bun, asked to see his passport. He glanced at me anxiously, but then he smiled as he withdrew his passport and offered it to the impatient lady.

I gazed up and sighed quietly, thanking my former high-school chum, the Honorable Bernie Rothenberg, for remaining the lackadaisical careless person he had always been. He hadn't required that Feig surrender his passport. In Bernie's defense, however, Carol hadn't thought of it either. And, given the nature of the crime and the age of the defendant, the last thing anyone was thinking the day bail was set was that he might leave the country. The possibility certainly had not crossed my mind when I used all my available cash to post his bail. How ironic, I thought, that the one with the most to lose concocted the scheme for Feig to flee to Israel.

What I counted on was that, under Israeli law, the Jewish nation was not compelled to honor requests for extradition from other countries. This is difficult for many people to understand, but the primary purpose of the founding of the modern state of Israel was to furnish a safety net for the millions of Jews living all over the globe whenever they found themselves persecuted. Israel would not only provide a refuge for Jews fleeing oppression, but it would also offer a haven for any Jew unjustly prosecuted. Sometimes it was obvious that a prosecution was a guise for persecution—as in the case of trials inspired by the blood libel or Jews in Arab countries accused of espionage. In other instances, the anti-Semitism was subtler.

To counter the argument that Jewish criminals would seek asylum in Israel, and in an effort to insure justice, the Jewish state retained the option of trying the defendant in a Jewish court of law where they would be judged by fellow Jews. While this was a risk for Feig, given the circumstances and the charges against him I saw a trial as highly unlikely and the possibility of a jail sentence practically unthinkable.

In any event, I doubted the question of extradition would even be raised since I couldn't imagine anyone looking all that hard for Feig in the first place. Besides Ilse's children, most of those involved would likely heave a collective sigh of relief that this controversial case had vanished into thin air.

There would, no doubt, be a wringing of hands in the District Attorney's Office and Judge Rothenberg, in stern consternation, would forfeit my bail. But that would be for show. Behind the curtain veiling American jurisprudence from the public eye, there would be mutterings of feeling sorry for that poor shmuck, David Gold, who got conned by a wily old man into losing the cash bail he posted. They would never know that the idea was mine, nor would they know that it had taken much convincing, cajoling, and badgering to get Feig to agree. Even then, he consented only after swearing to repay me—which we both knew was unlikely.

"The suitcase, David." Feig interrupted my reverie.

With a grunt, I lifted the baggage onto the platform to be weighed and tagged. The EL AL agent arched her eyebrows.

"You certainly packed this to the limit, Mr. Feeg," she said, mispronouncing his name. "Plan on staying long?"
Feig shot me a nervous glance and nodded as the woman tagged his suitcase and then slid his boarding pass over the counter.

We walked toward the waiting area in silence. We both knew that, despite what we might say to delude ourselves, it was unlikely we would ever see each other again.

The departure area was crammed with the same people who had been waiting in line at the ticket counter. But the tension was gone. No more anxiety about passing through customs or being charged for overweight baggage. All that remained was to board the Jewish plane serviced by a Jewish crew and, twelve hours later, to set foot on the soil of the first Jewish state in two millennia. I spotted the first-time visitors by the puffing of their chests and the swagger in their gait. They were proud to be claiming the Jewish homeland as their own.

When the boarding announcement came I felt a pounding in my chest. Feig and I looked at each other.
He spoke first. "David, what can I say that I haven't said already?" Tears were welling in his blue eyes. "Will you be OK?"

"Yes, I told you not to worry. I'll be fine."

"And I'll repay you."

"I know, and I don't what to hear about this again. Now, will you be all right?"

His eyes shifted for a moment to a spot just beyond my shoulder. Then he shrugged. "How could I not? I've been a survivor all my life. Much, much worse than this, you know."

I nodded.

"It is you, my friend, for whom I worry."

"Why?"

"Because, David, while you may be a survivor, you do not know how to survive."

"Jacob, I don't have a clue what you're talking about."

"It is this, my friend. You are a survivor, but you have never fully understood what it was you survived. With me, it was different. There was no question what I had to survive. I knew what I was facing—the Nazi camps and the genocide of the Jews. The world even gave us a special name—'Holocaust survivors.' Then I had to survive the wars in Israel. And then I had to survive the threat of prison and, thanks to you, I did—like a cat with nine lives!" He smiled, but then his face grew serious again. "But with you, David, it has not been this clear. Indeed, it has been so insidious that no one has recognized it or pointed it out to you or allowed you to discover it for yourself."

"And what may that be?"

"You had to survive us, David," he said.

I shook my head. I still had no idea what he was talking about.

"You had to grow up living not only in the shadow of the Holocaust, cast by the flames and ashes of six million dead Jews who went up in smoke, but you also had to navigate the wake left by the living—those like myself, like your grandparents—walking ghosts filling the hulls of crippled ships being towed to shore. Your shore, David, your world, your country, your home."

I looked at him long and hard, but it was not his face that I saw—only the soft blue eyes of my grandfather. And I cried.

Feig embraced me. We hugged. But we were not conspicuous. People all around us were embracing—some sobbing, knowing they would not see each other for months or years. But my tears did not arise from the present or from thoughts projected into the future. My tears were grounded in the past, and as they flowed and spilled down my cheeks, I was washed clean from the guilt I had borne for so long—the guilt that, somehow, I was to blame for the silent suffering of those I loved.

He pulled away, grinned, and laughed aloud.

"What is it, Jacob?"

"Life is sometimes like a circle, isn't it David? And so incredible. After all, here we stand, four decades later, and the grandson of the woman who rescued me so long ago is saving my life. What a world!" Feig laughed again.

I just shook my head and smiled.

Feig joined the line and disappeared from sight. I stood by the window watching until the plane withdrew from the gate and taxied toward the runway. That was the last time I saw Feig—soaring into the heavens like the mythical phoenix, purplish wings spanning and merging into the red-yellow light of the rising sun.

As the plane disappeared from sight into the azure sky, I felt as if an awesome weight had been lifted from my shoulders. My chest expanded as I inhaled a deep breath of freedom—freedom from the guilt I had unknowingly carried all my life. Freedom from the guilt that I should have done something to save the victims, to aid the survivors, to make my grandparents and my mother happy.

But it was all in the past and I could do nothing to change any of it. Even if I had known then what I had come to learn about what Oma and Opa and my mother endured, I could not have done much about it.

But here. Now. I had done something. And, because of that, I felt completely at peace as I stood peering into the clear cerulean sky. Feig was safe and on his way.

It took a few minutes to sink in that he was gone— that he had stepped out of my life. But we did remain in contact. We exchanged Jewish New Year cards, the occasional phone call, and letters. And later, as he neared the end of his life, we emailed each other.

But most enduring was what remained unspoken. The knowing silence between us. Yet, strangely enough, it was only after Feig died that I began to feel differently about this. I kept hearing his rasping voice. "David, it is time. It is time to speak the unspeakable. Give voice to the ineffable. You are a writer, you know." I could see his wry grin and sparkling blue eyes as he urged me on.

I could not resist. Once again, Feig set my life in motion. And he was correct, of course. I am a writer. And, because of Feig, I finally have something to write about.

Acknowledgements
The gestation period for *Feig* spanned a decade and was
punctuated by several year-long breaks due to deadlines for
other projects. The final manuscript emerged only after two
earlier versions, bearing different titles, had been abandoned.
Were it not for encouragement from readers, I suspect *Feig*
might have joined other novels I've forsaken. I will be forever
grateful to Kirsten, Ari, Joy, Cory, Frani, and David Wilson
for providing that support.

Having worked with scores of editors and publishers over the
years, I am not new to the editorial process. But the people
I've worked with at PS Books have brought skill, dedication
to quality, and insight into the essence of the work that I
do not recall experiencing elsewhere. My gratitude to my
editors Mary Ann Miller, Tara Smith, and especially to Carla
Spataro, who not only aided in the editing but also provided
the vote of confidence in acquiring the book.

About the Author
Richard D. Bank, Esq., is the author of six books, including
The Everything Guide to Writing Nonfiction (Adams Media,
2010). He is a past president of the Philadelphia Writers'
Conference and has published over one hundred articles,
essays, and short stories in various journals and periodicals.
He has taught writing courses at numerous venues, including
the University of Pennsylvania and Temple University, and is
currently on the faculty at Rosemont College in the Graduate
Publishing and MFA in Creative Writing programs. He also
provides services as a writer's coach. A lifelong resident of
the Philadelphia area, he lives in Upper Dublin with his wife
Francine. *Feig* is his first novel.

www.ingramcontent.com/pod-product-compliance
Lightning Source LLC
Chambersburg PA
CBHW060645260626
47161CB00008B/3011